Samuel Hulbeart Turner

Autobiography of the Rev. Samuel H. Turner

Late Professor of Biblical Learning and the Interpretation of Scripture

Samuel Hulbeart Turner

Autobiography of the Rev. Samuel H. Turner
Late Professor of Biblical Learning and the Interpretation of Scripture

ISBN/EAN: 9783337098438

Printed in Europe, USA, Canada, Australia, Japan

Cover: Foto ©Raphael Reischuk / pixelio.de

More available books at **www.hansebooks.com**

OF THE

REV. SAMUEL H. TURNER, D.D.,

LATE

PROFESSOR OF BIBLICAL LEARNING AND THE INTERPRETATION OF SCRIPTURE

IN THE

GENERAL THEOLOGICAL SEMINARY OF THE PROTESTANT EPISCOPAL CHURCH IN THE UNITED STATES OF AMERICA.

— — — • • • —

NEW-YORK:

A. D. F. RANDOLPH, 683 BROADWAY.

1864.

CONTENTS.

———•••———

PREFACE, ... ix

CHAPTER I.

Design of the Writer—Parentage—Early Associates—Studies—
College Course—Choice of a Profession—Visit to the Rev. Dr.
Feltus—Its Effect upon his Mind—He becomes a Communi-
cant in St. Paul's Church, Philadelphia, under the ministry of
Dr. Pilmore—Influence of Religious Books—Studies for the
Ministry under Bishop White—Text-books Employed—Adopts
the Views of Stillingfleet, Hooker and White in regard to
Church Polity—Avidity in Study—Mistakes Corrected—He-
brew and Greek Studies, ... 9–33

CHAPTER II.

Ordination—Revisits Dr. Feltus—Succeeds the Rev. Wm. H. Wilmer in Chestertown, Maryland—First Sermon there—Letter
from Judge Chambers respecting the "I. U. Church"—Character and Extent of his Labors—The Haunted House—Parochial Visiting—Labors among the Blacks—Weekly Lectures—Sermon-Writing—Theological, Ecclesiastical, and Biblical Studies—Latin and Greek Classics, and Hebrew Language
—Best Mode of Learning Ancient Languages—Important
Principle in the Composition of Sermons—Pioneer in the
Sunday-School Work—Election of Bishop Kemp—War with
England—Fight near Chestertown, . . . 34–56

CHAPTER III.

Pernicious Effects of Climate and Slavery—He is offered a Professorship at Annapolis—Leaves Chestertown—Call to Germantown, Pa.—St. Ann's, Brooklyn—Elizabeth, New-Jersey—Rev. Dr. Bowen—Grace Church, New-York—Dr. Jarvis—Return to Philadelphia—Visits Chestertown, Washington, and various places in Virginia, returning by Central Pennsylvania—His Mother's Death—Her Character—Historical and Theological Studies—Labors in Philadelphia—Trinity Church the Result—Preached the Opening Sermon,   .   .   .   57–69

CHAPTER IV.

Appointed Superintendent of the Theological School in Philadelphia—Bishop Alonzo Potter his first Pupil—Translation of "Bochart's Phaleg"—A General Theological Seminary Proposed in the General Convention—Measures Taken for its Establishment—History of its Formation and Organization—Mr. Turner Elected Professor of "Historic Theology"—Charged Temporarily with the Duties of the Professor of Systematic Theology—Dr. C. C. Moore's Gift to the Seminary –Rev. Dr. Gadsden's "Statement for the Seminary"—South-Carolina its Originator—The Error of the Bishop of Oxford in ascribing it to the Influence of Bishop Hobart—First Students in the Seminary—Professor Turner's Course of Instruction, ...   70–85

CHAPTER V.

Indifference of Bishop Hobart and leading New-York Clergymen to the Seminary—Proof of Want of Interest—Difficulties with Professor Jarvis—Professor Turner's Views on certain points of Theology not in Harmony with those of Bishop Hobart—The Seminary removed to New-Haven—Bishop Brownell's Remarks in regard to it—The Seminary organized on a New Plan—Open to Students of all Religious Denominations—Incidents of the Summer's Vacation—Introductory Discourse at New-Haven—Varied and Pleasant Duties in the Semi-

nary—Its Patrons and Friends—His Father's Death—Sketch
of his Life, ... 86–111

CHAPTER VI.

A Diocesan Theological School established in New-York, at the
Instance of Bishop Hobart—Jacob Sherred's Legacy—A Special General Convention called to consider it — The Seminary
restored to New-York—United with the Diocesan School under
a New Organization—Reörganization of the Seminary — First
Critical Publication—South-Carolina Trustees suggest a Seminary-Building—Bishop White's Remarks on laying the Corner-
Stone—Professor Turner's Marriage — Progress and Character
of the Seminary Buildings—Study of the French and German
Languages—Revision of our Church Psalmody and Hymns—
Translation of "Jahn's Introduction," with Notes — Birth of
his First Child — Establishment of Public Worship at the
Seminary—Formation of a Sunday-School—St. Peter's Church
grows out of these Labors—Studies in Ancient and Modern
Languages, and in Rabbinical Writings—Dr. Nordheimer,
112–132

CHAPTER VII.

Clerical Association in New-York—Object of it — Constitution
— Bishop Hobart's Attack upon it — Dr. Turner's Reply—
The Course pursued by the Members — Erroneous Impres-
sions—Essays, etc., in Biblical Literature, . . 133–168

CHAPTER VIII.

Elected Professor of Hebrew Language in Columbia College—
Lectures in the College Chapel—Their Publication—Discour-
agements — Death of his Daughter — Translation and Publication of Professor Planck's Introduction to Theological
Knowledge, with Notes — Birth of his first Son — Peter G.
Stuyvesant's Endowment of a Professorship in the Seminary — Death of Mrs. Turner — Publication of "Companion to
the Book of Genesis"—Object of the Work—Criticisms of two
Church Papers, ... 169–183

CHAPTER IX.

History of the Seminary—New-York City an Unfavorable Location—Effects of the Doctrines of the Oxford Tracts and their kindred Usages — Conflicting Views with regard to them — Suggestion of the Examining Committee — Dissent of Drs. Anthon and Smith, in the Committee — Professor Turner's Reply to the Implied Censure—The true Place and Value of the Early Fathers in the Exposition of Scripture—A Proposition to the Trustees—Resolutions of the South-Carolina Convention — Unfavorable Rumors in regard to the Seminary—Report of the South-Carolina Committee—Singular Questions propounded to the Faculty—Episcopal Visitation of the Seminary — Professor Turner's Answers — Communication from Bishop McIlvaine—Christmas Novelties—Apostasies to Rome — Professor Turner's Resistance to Novelties — The Attempt of "The Churchman" to Ridicule his Published Statement of Facts—"Records of Councils"—Its Ignorance and Indecency —Resolutions of the Visiting Bishops — The Real Value of their Opinion—Romanism among the Students—Secret Plans for Propagating it—Action of the Faculty—Expulsions from the Seminary—The Expelled Students Ordained in New-York, North-Carolina and Maryland — Further Apostasies to Rome —Influences Outside of the Seminary—The Errors and Cant Phrases of the Times — Characters most easily led astray — The Responsibility of those who Recommend Candidates for Orders — Resignation of Professors Wilson and Moore—Professor Ogilby's Death — Appointment of Professor Johnson and Mahan, ...   184–213

CHAPTER X.

Serious Personal Injury—Record of Publications—"Essay on our Lord's Discourse at Capernaum"—"Biographical Notices of Jewish Rabbis"—Dr. Murdock's opinion of the Work—"Spiritual Things Compared with Spiritual"—Reply to Strictures upon the Publication—Two Discourses on the Rule of Faith— A Volume on Prophecy—The Epistle to the Hebrews in Greek

and English—The Epistle to the Romans in Greek and English—The Epistle to the Ephesians in Greek and English—The
Epistle to the Galatians in Greek and English, . 214–234

CHAPTER XI.

Plain-Song in the Seminary—Mr. Hopkins—Pastoral Care of
the Students—The American Bible Society—His Relation
to it—The Standard Bible—The Fortieth Anniversary of his
Professorship—Sketch of Dr. Wilson—General Review,

235–266

CHAPTER XII.

EDITORIAL CONCLUSION.

Death—Funeral—Bishop Potter's Address—Notices of the Press
—Resolution of various Committees, etc., . . 267–292

PREFACE.

———•◆•———

THE following autobiography of the Rev. Dr. Turner does not contain all the important events of his life, much less does it present the striking features of his character. As a memoir, a delineation of the whole man, or as a history, it is incomplete.

The main design of the writer was, to leave for his family, a memorial of the principles which governed his conduct, and of those events which would be especially interesting to them; and to furnish an authentic record of such facts connected with his official and public life as he deemed particularly important to the truth of history, the cause of the Gospel and of sacred learning.

The work of the editor has been limited to the breaking up of the narrative into chapters, preparing suitable headings, appending a few pages at the conclusion, and superintending the progress of the book through the press.

For several years he has enjoyed the friendship of the lamented author, and regards it a special privilege and honor to be connected with the publication of this sketch of his life.

May the illustrious example of one so gifted, quietly and unostentatiously prosecuting his arduous work, employing with marked diligence and devotion the many talents committed to his trust, adhering through a protracted life so inflexibly to the " old paths" of truth, and, by his life and conversation, adorning the doctrine of God his Saviour, incite others, and especially those who, as learners, were privileged to sit at his feet, to follow him even as he followed Christ.

E. H. C.

Brooklyn, May 6th, 1863.

AUTOBIOGRAPHY

OF THE

REV. SAMUEL H. TURNER, D.D.

———•◦•———

CHAPTER I.

Design of the Writer—Parentage—Early Associates—Studies—College Course—Choice of a Profession—Visit to the Rev. Dr. Feltus—Its Effect upon his Mind—He becomes a Communicant in St. Paul's Church, Philadelphia, under the ministry of Dr. Pilmore—Influence of Religious Books—Studies for the Ministry under Bishop White—Text-books Employed—Adopts the Views of Stillingfleet, Hooker and White in regard to Church Polity—Avidity in Study—Mistakes Corrected—Hebrew and Greek Studies.

THE following notice of some particulars of my life is committed to writing in the belief that my children will feel an interest in a brief sketch of their father's biography, however imperfect, and in the hope that they will not fail to trace the hand of Divine Providence in directing and moulding apparently incidental circumstances, so as to promote His own wise and

1*

benevolent purposes. With the exception of what peculiarly constitutes the Gospel of our Lord Jesus Christ, and is essentially connected with the plan of redemption through Him, the only Mediator, there is no principle more satisfactory, and in its influence on human character and action more practical, than that which recognizes the agency of God in all events of life, however seemingly unimportant. The exercise of a steady and habitual faith in this doctrine will enable a man to submit with acquiescence at least, if not with cheerfulness, to the dispensations of Heaven, and to trust the universal Ruler even when His arrangements appear to be at variance with His general course of kindness, confident that the result will afford evidence both of His wisdom and also of His benevolence.

I was born on the twenty-third of January, 1790, in the house of my father, the Rev. Joseph Turner, No. 370 South Second Street, in the District of Southwark, Philadelphia. My mother, . whose name was Elizabeth Mason, was the daughter of a physician of Devonshire, England, of which country my father also was a native. The mansion was built by his uncle, Philip Hulbeart, who occupied it as his country-seat a long time before the revolutionary war. The gradual increase of the city soon brought the dwelling within the limits of regular streets, numerous houses, and a considerable population; although, when I was a boy, there were extensive fields in the vicinity, some of which were under cultivation, and others, lying low, were covered with water, affording, in winter, fine skating-places. The house was solidly built of brick, and was occupied by the family for more than one hundred years. My father always retained a large space of ground in two divisions, which were respectively appropriated to flower and vegetable gardens. The cultivation of these he superintended himself, an employment which was a source of great gratification to him even in advanced age. His early vegetables, fine fruit of various kinds, particularly cherries, and beautiful display of roses, and other flowers, were, in the beginning of summer, a general attraction to the neighborhood. Among the earliest recollections of my childhood are his faithful black dog, Bull, a necessary guard, especially during the long winter nights, and a sorrel horse, Jack, which for twenty years carried him in his chaise, to his country churches, and was a well-trained and sagacious favorite.

I was the youngest of eight children, three

sons and five daughters. My eldest brother, after whom I received my first name, died before I was born, and the other, named after his parents Joseph Mason, who was two and a half years older than myself, died at about the age of twenty-two. At the time of my birth my father was forty-eight years old. He died on the twenty-sixth of July, 1821, at the age of seventy-nine.

Of the period of my childhood I have nothing of much consequence to relate. I remember showing my copy-book to my father's old friend, the Rev. Dr. Blackwell, one summer afternoon, in 1796, and about the same time being called up in Mr. Little's school, that my father, who happened to make a visit there, might hear me read in the New Testament. The portion selected was the first part of the thirteenth chapter of St. Mark, and I well recollect how strange and incomprehensible the statement in the second verse appeared to me. I could not see how " one stone" should " not be left upon another," and yet should " not be thrown down." I remember having been ill with the yellow fever in 1798, when all our family except our parents suffered with the disease. The only particulars which I can call to mind are, that the attack commenced at night, with a violent chill and pains in the back and head, and that at some period of the sickness my father spoke to me about dying, and preparation for another world, from which I infer that I must have been seriously ill. A servant-girl died of the complaint in our house, also Mr. George Keppele, who within a year before had been married to my sister Ann. I mention as a very remarkable fact, that although our own family physician, Dr. Pfeiffer, a German of the Moravian Church, was too unwell to leave his house, my father being obliged to visit him daily and report our respective cases, and bring home his prescriptions, yet all his patients, with the exception of the servant before alluded to, recovered of that deadly distemper. Mr Keppele had the personal attendance of another physician. The doctor's son, who not long after became a medical student in Philadelphia, gave evidence of more than ordinary ability and industry, and would no doubt have become distinguished in his profession had he not been cut off by an early death.

My first Latin teacher was the Rev. John Melancthon Bradford. He was a nephew of the venerable Dr. Ashbel Green, at that time a celebrated Presbyterian clergyman in Phila-

delphia, and afterwards President of Princeton
College. He was also the father of Alexander
W. Bradford, LL.D., the able jurist who is now
Surrogate of New-York. He became a clergyman of the Dutch Church, and settled in Al-
bany. On his leaving the city I was put under the care of Mr. James Thompson, who two
or three years afterwards became Professor of
Languages in the University of Pennsylvania.
He taught in the Quaker Academy in Fourth
street near Chestnut, which at that time was
one of the best Latin schools in the city. The
whole time was devoted to the ancient languages, except half an hour employed in writing a copy and listening to a chapter in the
Bible read by all the scholars in rotation.
The morning was spent in reciting; one lesson
in Greek or Latin Grammar; one in Cæsar,
Sallust, or Virgil, and I think after the study
of Greek was begun, we had another in the
Gospel of St. John, or Lucian. A single lesson in some one of these authors occupied the
afternoon. The Academy was patronized by
some of the best families. Dallas, now our
minister at the Court of St. James, was one of
its pupils. The late Thomas I. Wharton, well
known and esteemed as a highly respectable
member of the Philadelphia bar, was one of

my class-mates. We entered the University of Pennsylvania in January, 1806, and graduated together on July twenty-third, 1807, when I was exactly seventeen and a half years old. Our whole collegiate period did not exceed eighteen months. The University was at that time in a very depressed condition. There were then but two classes, the Junior and the Senior. Although I entered the former at nearly its middle period, I had so far forgotten my arithmetic that I was obliged to begin with reduction or the rule of three. The course was necessarily very imperfect, although the institution commanded the services of some very able men, especially the literary and classical Dr. Andrews, Vice-Provost, and the elder Dr. Patterson, distinguished for his knowledge of mathematics and philosophy. The learned John McDowell, LL.D., entered upon his duties as Provost only a few months before I left. He used to say that Bishop White and Dr. James Wilson were the two clergymen whom he habitually heard with satisfaction.

Our mathematical studies comprehended the elements of algebra, the first four books of Euclid, plane and spherical trigonometry, surveying, gauging, and navigation. Some of the class, I think, learned conic sections. I know that I copied out the elements of this branch, but never studied the subject. One member, Mr. Joseph Hall, son of a former Governor of Delaware, who was decidedly head of the class, rose above us all into the regions of fluxions; but I believe he soared alone in this high atmosphere of mathematics. Chemistry, mineralogy, and other similar branches, were entirely ignored. A slight course of mechanics, hydraulics, hydrostatics, optics, and astronomy constituted the sum of our instruction in natural philosophy. In moral, Beattie's Elements was the only text-book; in history, the Abbé Millot; in rhetoric and logic, Dr. Andrews's Compends. Our Latin reading embraced Horace, Cicero's Orations and De Officiis, and two or three Satires of Juvenal. In Greek we read some Dialogues of Lucian, two books of the Cyropædia, three of Homer, Epictetus, and some portions of Longinus. I never wrote a page of English composition either at school or college. The oration which I delivered at Commencement was furnished by a friend; and about two weeks afterwards I had the gratification of seeing it in a periodical some three or four months old!

I left college without any determination as to my future course of life. I knew that my parents were desirous that I should devote myself to the ministry. But they never made use of any persuasion, or attempted to bias my mind towards the sacred profession. In early youth my thoughts and feelings were often under strong religious influence; and I remember, when a mere child, going into a small closet to pray. But I have no reason to believe that these impressions were very deep or habitual in their influence. My deportment had always been morally correct, and I had a good deal of conscientiousness. But when the question of the choice of an occupation or profession came up for consideration, my mind wavered, and I became very undecided. I can not say that I felt any ardent, earnest desire to make known to others the Gospel, because of having myself experienced its blessings. In this doubtful state of mind, I was at one time strongly inclined to study medicine under the direction of Dr. Benjamin Rush, who had been for some years our family physician, and had repeatedly prescribed for frequent indispositions, to which in early life I was subject. I had unfortunately become quite experienced in his ten or twenty grains' prescriptions of calomel and jalap, taken to remove some trifling ailment, or in the spring, when I was enjoying good health, to keep off the enemy who was supposed to be insidiously lurking in ambush. Happily I was not subjected to bleeding or cupping; though, from frequent observation, I became familiar enough with the former.

While thus wavering in the choice of a profession, I accepted an invitation from a clerical friend of my father to spend a week with him at his parsonage in Swedesborough, New-Jersey. I found the Rev. Henry J. Feltus very kind and hospitable. He treated me like a younger brother, or rather like a son. And here I can not but say a few words in reference to this truly pious and good man, to whom I am greatly indebted. Mr. Feltus was a kind-hearted and devoted pastor. It was evidently his great object to do good among the people of his charge.. He well knew how to accommodate himself to their generally plain habits and mode of living, so as to make his association with them practically available to their spiritual good. He was exceedingly pleasant in his private intercourse, told a story admirably, and relished a good witticism as well as any man I ever knew. Although his early education had been imperfect, and his acquaintance with literature and science was limited, yet he had evidently read much, and acquired considerable information. In the pulpit he was at times quite eloquent—disposed, however, to introduce occasionally some show of learning. His discourses were characterized by sound Scriptural instruction, and an evident desire to impress religious truths upon the understandings and hearts of his people. He was deservedly much respected and beloved. I became very intimate with, and greatly attached to him. I accompanied him on some of his parochial visits. One occasion of this kind made a strong impression on my mind. Having made his personal preparations, in doing which it was his habit to be rather particularly attentive as to his dress and appearance, he took me into his study, and, after locking the door, kneeled down and offered a short prayer for divine aid and guidance. We rode to the houses of several of his parishioners, some of whom were hard-working, industrious poor; and to all he had some religious counsel, or instruction, or exhortation to give, generally closing his pastoral visit with a short and fervent prayer. The tendency of his mind seemed to be to depend on God and to ask His aid. On another occasion, a walk of a considerable distance having brought us into a deep and retired wood, he suddenly stopped short and said, "Let us improve this scene;" and kneeling down among the thick trees, where no eye of man was likely to observe us, he poured out a prayer to the "Father who seeth in secret." He was fond of, and slightly acquainted with, music. I spent a pleasant and profitable week with this excellent clergyman, and freely opened my mind to him respecting my uncertainty as to the profession I should choose. He did not advise me to form an immediate resolution to enter the sacred ministry, knowing that this ought to be the result of a conviction of duty arising out of a desire to make known the Gospel as the only method of salvation for sinners; and, considering my youth and inexperience, his counsel was, to begin a course of theological reading, and to defer any determination in the matter to a subsequent period, when I should be better able than I was at that time to make a right decision. If this should not be in favor of entering upon the sacred office, the course of reading pursued would yet be useful, and I should still have sufficient time to make suitable preparation for another profession. On my return home I took his advice, and adopted the course recommended.

During the following autumn my religious

views and feelings became enlarged and deepen-
ed. My convictions of man's natural sinfulness,
of the need of a Redeemer to reconcile sinful
man to his Maker, of a Divine agency to turn
the heart to heavenly things, of self-devotion
to God, and a holy life, became stronger; and
I pursued my theological reading with a direct
view to ultimate admission into the ministry of
the Church. This state of mind was, in a considerable degree, promoted by the conversation
and counsel of Mr. George Warner, who afterwards married my elder sister, the widow of
Mr. Keppele. Mr. Warner's son, a married
gentleman with three children, was residing in
the neighborhood of Philadelphia, where he
had gone for the benefit of country air adapted
to his condition. He was gradually sinking in
consumption, of which disease he died not long
after. I accompanied Mr. Warner one morning, I think in October, to the sick man's residence, and for the first time partook with him
of the holy communion, administered by the
Rev. Mr. Feltus, of whom Mr. Warner had
been an old friend and patron. Afterwards I
became a communicant in St. Paul's Church, to
which our family belonged — then under the
charge of the Rev. Joseph Pilmore, D.D., who
had succeeded Dr. Samuel Magaw as rector.

The work which was most effective, in the Providence of God, in opening and impressing my mind in reference to practical religion, was Doddridge's *Rise and Progress of Religion in the Soul.* Few books have been more extensively blessed to the conversion of the sinner and the edification of the Christian, than this unpretending, simple, and earnest production of one of the kindest, most intelligent, useful, and holy men of modern times. To this work I must add, as one of the most deeply religious books ever published, Bishop Beveridge's *Private Thoughts.* This very practical treatise I found greatly beneficial; and, indeed, it can hardly be too highly prized. It ought to be familiar to every Christian, and especially to every one who aspires to the sacred ministry of the Church.

My theological studies were pursued under the direction of Bishop White, whom I regularly visited in his study, at first once in two weeks, and afterwards once a month, for upwards of three years. The Bishop never subjected me to any examinations; indeed, I do not recollect that he ever questioned me in reference to any theological point except at my examinations for orders. If the plan of stated recitations had been pursued with some regularity, my studies would, no doubt, have been more thorough and my knowledge more accurate. As it was, I read a great deal, but thought and studied little. To use common language, I crammed so fully that I had neither opportunity nor ability to digest any thing intellectually. Consequently, my conceptions of theology as a system were very vague and undefined, and my acquaintance with the several departments of divinity loose and imperfect. The candor of the good Bishop showed itself in one respect, very conspicuously, illustrating also his love of truth and his confidence that a search after it was best promoted, not by concealment of error, but by general and extended investigation of controverted points. If he recommended any one book in defense of doctrine or discipline, he did not hesitate to put into my hands some other defending an opposite view. Thus Campbell's Lectures on Ecclesiastical History were read in connection with Skinner's Truth and Order, and Lord King's Primitive Church along with Slater's Original Draft. After Hooker's Ecclesiastical Polity, and Potter on Church Government, with the controversial works of Hobart, Howe, Bowden, and Miller, he put into my hand, Stillingfleet's Irenicum.

And I shall never forget the remark which he then made: " A book much spoken against, but never answered."*

I read somewhat extensively on the subject of Church polity. For a considerable time my mind was unsettled, and I studied the various

---

* When a young man, I heard it said by some of our elderly and most distinguished clergymen, that Stillingfleet retracted in after-life the principles of this book. I never met with any one, however, who could tell me where this retraction was to be found, though I repeatedly made the inquiry. I can not believe that he ever retracted the fundamental principles of the book, which, indeed, are very like, and in a measure identical with those of Hooker. No doubt he changed his views on some of the details, and especially in what he says on the subject, of ordination by presbyters. And probably the rumor above alluded to, had its origin in the following passages which occur in the author's preface to his Unreasonableness of Separation, quarto, London, 1682. When he published this work he was Dean of St. Paul's ; twenty years before, when the Irenicum made its appearance, he was rector of Sutton, in Bedfordshire. On a public occasion the Dean had preached a sermon on "the unreasonableness and mischief of the present separation." This production became the occasion of a good deal of controversy, and, among other things, the preacher was charged with advocating views inconsistent with those which he had maintained in the Irenicum. In reply he makes the following acknowledgments implied or expressed : " Will you not allow a person who happened to write about these matters when he was very young, in twenty years' time of the most busy and thoughtful part of his life, to see reason to alter his judgment? But after all, where is it that he hath thus contradicted himself? Is it in the point of separation ? No," etc. " But if any thing in the following treatise," that is, the work on Separation, "be found different from the sense of that book, I do entreat them to allow me that which I heartily wish to them, namely, that in *twenty years'* time we may arrive to such maturity of thought as to see reason to change our opinion of *some things*, and I wish I had not cause to add of *some persons* too." (Pp. lxxii. lxxvi.) But these passages afford very insufficient grounds for the statement that the author retracted the principles of his former work

works with particular attention. The result of my examination was this, that diocesan Episcopacy was of apostolic origin, instituted under divine guidance, and consequently *jure divino.* But whether this form of church government was divinely established in perpetuity, and intended to be necessary to the Church at all periods, so that the preservation of it becomes essential to its existence, or whether it were established as being best adapted to the apostolic age, so that, subsequently, changes might be introduced without destroying the validity of the ministry or its acts; these appeared to be questions for private judgment, on which different views might allowably be entertained by different minds without affecting the soundness of their church views. The fact that the Jewish succession in the high priestly office had been tampered with, and persons introduced into it who had no legal Mosaic claim, and yet that in our Lord's time the Hebrew Church was not regarded as nullified or mutilated thereby, nor the ecclesiastical authority of those who thus held office questioned by Him, but that on the contrary, He spoke of the Scribes and Pharisees as "sitting in Moses' seat," and therefore having a rightful claim to obedience, made a strong impression on me,

2

and had no slight influence in enabling me to come to a decision. The principle defended against the Puritans by Hooker,* that even divinely established laws are not necessarily permanent, was that on which my mind ultimately rested. I saw no reason for abandoning Episcopacy, but on the contrary very strong ones for adhering to it. Yet I could not admit the conclusion that those who had done so, had thereby unchurched themselves, especially under circumstances where Episcopacy could not readily be secured.

I read, in manuscript, most of the Bishop's Calvinistic and Armenian controversy, which had not then been published. The reference in that work to Calvin's early view of the meaning of 1 Pet. 2 : 8, " Whereunto also they were appointed," which he originally considered as expressive of " the favorable circumstances in which the Jews were placed for their reception of the Gospel," was suggested by me at that time. Not long before, I had purchased at the sale of a portion of the library of the Rev. Dr. Kunze, (a Lutheran clergyman, who had been professor of Hebrew in Columbia College,) a copy of Gerhard's Loci Theologici, where I found the pas-

* Eccles. Polity, Book III. sections 9, 10.'

sage to which the Bishop refers, and pointed it out to him.

During the period of nearly three and a half years which I spent in reading divinity under Bishop White, attention was habitually given to the sacred Scriptures. I read Patrick, Stackhouse's History of the Bible, Whitby, Doddridge's Expositor, Campbell on the Gospels, consulted Poole's Annotations and such other books as I had access to. Indeed, at one period of the course I got together all the commentators I could procure, had them opened and arrranged on a large table, and read one after the other with persevering industry until I became tired and bewildered. The result was a confused jumble of information, often inconsistent, sometimes positively contradictory; and vague, indefinite, unsatisfactory notions of the meaning. I learned by experience that no clear perception of the oracles of God was attainable in this way. I was incompetent to form a judgment respecting the truth among diversified and opposing expositions, and the views of one respectable commentator were received as sufficiently satisfactory until the conflicting views of the next in order suggested difficulties that weakened or destroyed the impressions which had been made by the former. To which I add that in many cases none of them gave satisfactory expositions. With the principles of sacred criticism and interpretation I had no acquaintance. The idea of settling the true text of the Bible by referring to written authorities of manuscripts, versions, and quotations, a thousand years or more older than the invention of printing, had never occurred to me. Of Mill, Wetstein, or Griesbach, I had never heard. Interpretation as a science was almost equally unknown, and when I felt difficulties in certain expositions maintained by orthodox annotators of reputation, or failed to get from them any clear instruction, I attributed this want of satisfaction to my inability fully to comprehend the points in question, admitting the correctness and sufficiency of the expositions as a matter of course, because they had the *imprimatur* of authority. Having been brought up in the church of which Dr. Pilmore was the rector, I imbibed, in general, the leading doctrines which were there preached, and with which those that I had been accustomed to hear at home coincided. The views of Romaine, Hervey, Newton, and others of the same school were regarded with great deference, and I well remember that I considered the denial of the direct imputation of Christ's active obedience to the believer as the sole ground of his justification, as an abandonment of a fundamental truth of Christianity. The texts in St. Paul's Epistles which were thought to be conclusive in favor of this point, have since that time been carefully examined, and I am satisfied that they do not teach the doctrine.

After some time my attention was turned more particularly than before to the study of the Greek Testament. I bought Parkhurst's Lexicon, fourth edition, octavo, 1804, congratulating myself on having secured for nine dollars and fifty cents the greatest Biblical treasure of the sort which had ever appeared. I studied his introductory Greek grammar, and made myself familiar with the paradigms of the verbs so far as they are given in his work. It need not surprise you to be told that although I had graduated at the University, I could not inflect a Greek verb, and had no clear conception of the peculiar force of the middle voice, or of the distinction between the aorist and perfect tenses. Notwithstanding all the boasted improvements in the education of the present day, parallel cases are now not at all uncommon. Not a few young men have I found, fresh from college, with diplomas in their hands, who could not read, parse, and translate half a dozen verses in the Gospels with any thing like accuracy. Indeed, I have known graduates, respectable in general acquaintance with Latin and Greek, who could not thoroughly translate and parse the first four verses of St. Luke's Gospel. Parkhurst's verbs, however, I mastered, and set about a careful study of the New Testament in Greek, with the aid of his Lexicon. And although the book is now in a good degree superseded by others more profound and accurate, and although the author makes both it and his Hebrew Lexicon vehicles to convey to the student his Hutchinsonian notions, yet I must honestly acknowledge my great obligation to this good and learned man for the important aid that his work afforded me. Bishop Marsh's translation of the introduction of John David Michaelis, which I got from London through a friend of my father residing there, made me acquainted with the various points of New Testament criticism ; and Lightfoot's Horæ Hebraicæ et Talmudicæ brought to my notice the vast importance of Jewish literature in illustrating Scriptural phraseology.

After pursuing, for some time, the study of the Greek Testament, I adopted a practice which experience proved to be very useful. I accustomed myself to translate from English into Greek. In this way, I became the more familiar with the original text, so that before long I was able to use an English New Testament in church, and to read to myself in Greek, the lessons in the Gospels, after the officiating clergyman. Thus there became impressed on my memory many expressions, and even verses, of the Greek Testament, some of which it has retained to the present day. I regret that I did not carry out the principle, and, like that "right learned and godly man," Bishop Andrews, commit to memory the whole book.

A year or more before receiving deacons' orders, I commenced the study of Hebrew. The Rev. Samuel B. Wylie, at that time teacher of Latin and Greek in the University of Pennsylvania, was my instructor. Unfortunately, he was decidedly in favor of the system adopted by Masclef, Wilson, Parkhurst, and some others, and attempted to teach the language without points, employing the *matres lectiones* as vowels, and introducing a short *e* wherever the concurrence of two consonants required some sound to be expressed for which the letters of the word did not provide. In the course of a few months, I thought I was making rapid progress in the language. The Masoretical system of vowel-points appeared to me not only entirely useless, but a mass of confusion, a troublesome and traditionary excrescence, marring the simple beauty of the sacred tree of divine knowledge. I continued reading Hebrew in this way, with the assistance of Parkhurst's Lexicon, for six or seven years, until I had gone through by far the greater part of the Bible. But the result was a vague and indefinite knowledge. I had to consult a translation in order to ascertain whether a word was a noun or adjective or verb; and if the last, whether in a participial form, or preterite, or imperative, or infinitive, and whether it required an active or passive sense, and was or was not intensive in meaning. From the text alone, I could scarcely ever come to a definite conclusion in cases of difficulty. And such, I presume, must be the experience of all who confine themselves to this system.

My examination for orders was to myself very unsatisfactory, and, I think, it could not have been otherwise to the examiners. I had never been accustomed to examine myself on what I had read, nor had I before been at all subjected to examination on theological points by others. A good deal of reading without much thought, had left my mind poorly disciplined. I had a general idea of the various topics on which the examination turned, but was not able to develop them clearly, for want of the habit of reflecting on, of analyzing, and of stating propositions definitely. A consciousness of this incapacity was an advantage to me in after-life.

2*

CHAPTER II.

Ordination—Revisits Dr. Feltus—Succeeds the Rev. Wm. H. Wilmer in Chestertown, Maryland—First Sermon there—Letter from Judge Chambers respecting the " I. U. Church "—Character and Extent of his Labors—The Haunted House—Parochial Visiting—Labors among the Blacks—Weekly Lectures—Sermon-Writing—Theological, Ecclesiastical, and Biblical Studies—Latin and Greek Classics, and Hebrew Language —Best Mode of Learning Ancient Languages—Important Principle in the Composition of Sermons—Pioneer in the Sunday-School Work—Election of Bishop Kemp—War with England—Fight near Chestertown.

I was admitted to deacon's orders in St. Paul's Church, Philadelphia, on the morning of the twenty-seventh of January, 1811, being twenty-one years and four days old. The Rev. Dr. Pilmore, the rector, presented me. I preached my first sermon in the afternoon of the same day, at Christ Church. Like most young men, I was rather desirous to deliver a carefully prepared discourse, than simply to announce the glad tidings of salvation through Christ, although this point was not omitted. The text was the middle clause of John 3 : 19 : " Light is come into the world." After stating in the exordium the important principles, " that God does nothing in vain, and that, when necessary, He never fails to act," I proceeded to apply the latter axiom. It was my object to show, first, the necessity of a revelation from a view of religion and morals in the heathen world, previous to and at the time of the coming of Jesus Christ; secondly, to prove the truth of the position in the text, or to justify the assertion that "Light has come into the world;" and, thirdly, "from taking a comparative view of Heathenism and Christianity, to evince the infinite superiority of the latter." You will readily perceive, that in an address to a Christian audience, much of the matter discussed might have been regarded as admitted. The only good which could be expected to result, was the confirmation of previously existing faith.

I spent the greater part of the year 1811 at home, officiating occasionally in the city churches. In the course of the summer, I made a visit to New-York. I passed some weeks in New-Jersey — in Swedesborough, Glastenbury, and that vicinity. The Rev. Simon Wilmer, the successor of Mr. Feltus in Swedesborough, had, for a considerable time, been a frequent visitor at my father's. I spent some weeks at his house, and frequently preached and lectured in his parish. In this way, I became intimately acquainted with his brother, the Rev. William H. Wilmer, clergyman of the Church at Chestertown, Kent county, eastern shore of Maryland. There I made him a visit, preached in his church, and was introduced to some leading members of his congregation. He was then paying his addresses to Miss Marion Cox, of Mount Holly, N. J., and some time in the following January, I became his attendant on the occasion of his marriage. Just before this event, he had accepted an invitation to the church at Alexandria, Virginia, and I had been invited to become his successor at Chestertown. Early in 1812, I entered upon the duties of this parish, in connection with that of St. Paul's, eight miles farther down the county, the two having been for some time associated under one clergyman. My engagement was to officiate alternately every other Sunday morning in each church. My first sermon as pastor was preached on the morning of February sixteenth. It was a rainy day, and the congregation was small. I repeated it in St. Paul's, March twenty-second, to a larger audience. The words in 2 Cor. 5 : 20, " We are ambassadors for Christ," were selected as the text, and the subject was considered in the following order: First, the embassy or message itself; secondly, the persons to whom it should be announced; and thirdly, the manner in which it should be delivered. The embassy was stated to be the Gospel, the nature of which was explained and developed. The idea of delivering, in every discourse the general system of its doctrine was distinctly disavowed. It was stated that different points would be presented in different discourses; also, what the points were which a right announcement of the Gospel necessarily involved, from the fall of man to his ultimate restoration in everlasting life by means of the only one Mediator, Jesus, and the sanctifying influence of the Spirit of Grace. With regard to the second point, it was shown that to all classes of persons, beginning with the most daring infidel, and comprehending all sorts of sinners and worldly-minded, to believers also of every description, the ambassador of Christ had his appropriate message, every part of which he was to draw from his authoritative document, THE WORD OF GOD. Thirdly, it was stated that the minister of Christ must deliver his embassy with fidelity, not corrupting the message, or announcing it imperfectly; with earnestness, on account of its vast importance, and with love, as characteristic of its Author. The discourse was concluded by requesting the prayers of the congregation for the pastor whom the providence of God had called to labor among them.

The parish church of Chestertown was not the building in the town itself. It was situated about five miles north-west of it, and called I. U. Church. I endeavored repeatedly to ascertain the meaning of these initials, but never found any one, during my residence in Maryland, who could decipher it. My old friend and former parishioner, the Honorable Ezekiel F. Chambers, of Chestertown, to whom I lately applied for information, states as follows: "It is quite remarkable that no tradition has brought down to the present, or, as far as I can learn, the past generation, the slightest explanation or history of the name. (The Parish Register was destroyed piece-meal by the culpable neglect of those who should have preserved it.) This was partly occasioned by the fact that it continued to be the parish church after our chapel was erected in this place, and long after it ceased to claim a regular worshipping congregation, even after its entire dilapidation. When I was a member of the State Senate, I had an act of assembly passed making our town church the parish church. Until then some few of us were accustomed to ride out to I. U. on every Easter Monday to elect a vestry. I have partially examined our old records, and although I find no direct allusion to the church's name, I find what to my mind is a satisfactory solution. It is ascertained by reference to ancient deeds on record, that there was a family in the vicinity surnamed '*Ulrick*,' and among them a '*John Ulrick*.' It is also known that the cross-roads which have always run there were known by the name of I. U. cross-roads. The place probably took the same name, and also the church." As a similar case Judge Chambers adduces that " of a village in Queen Anne's, called J. B., from John Brown, the owner of the adjoining territory."

The church, which was known by this unusual name, was very old, greatly decayed, indeed almost dilapidated, and had not been used for sacred purposes for many years. On summer afternoons I often made appointments to preach there. The pulpit and desk were destroyed, so I used to accommodate myself by placing the door of one broken pew horizontally on the sides of another, selecting a spot where no loose portions of the ceiling threatened to fall, nor openings in the roof to let in a passing shower, and, arranging the Bible and prayer-book upon the hastily made lectern, I performed divine service and preached to the people of the surrounding country This church, I am informed, has lately been repaired. This is true also of one in the upper part of the county in Shrewsbury, and of St. Paul's in the lower part. These, with several others on the Eastern Shore, were put in good order under the Episcopal supervision of the present energetic diocesan. The sight of many large and fine church edifices suffered to go to ruin was very melancholy. In some places a small brick building had been erected a few rods from the church to serve as a vestry-room, and here divine services were occasionally held. I recollect riding with an old and much valued friend, the Rev. Henry Lyon Davis, seventeen miles on a week-day to a church in Caroline county on the border of Queen Anne's, where an appointment had been made. The church was found to be demolished except the walls, and its appearance gave too sure indications that it had been used for a long time as a shelter and stable for sheep and other cattle. The assembled congregation amounted to nine grown people, and four or five children. I very foolishly remarked to my reverend friend, that it would be ridiculous to preach to so few people; to which he very wisely replied, that it would be far more ridiculous not to preach to them.

Although the crumbling edifice of I. U. was the parish church, yet that in the town, to which no particular name was appropriated, was always practically so regarded. There, during the time of my residence in Maryland, elections of wardens and vestrymen were annually held, and other church business transacted. The congregation was not very large, but quite respectable in general character and intelligence, some of its members having, since that time, become distinguished both in Church and State. I was always treated with kindness and respect; and during my residence I cultivated some friendships which will not terminate even with death, but I trust, will, after that event, become settled and immutable.

On establishing myself at Chestertown, 1 began house-keeping with my sister Eliza. We occupied the same building in which my predecessor had lived, a country place of the Wilmer family, a short distance from the town, near the banks of a creek which emptied half a mile off into the Chester river. The family burial-ground was within about one hundred yards of the house, which had the unenviable distinction of being haunted ; and, as I afterwards learned, I acquired the reputation of laying the ghosts by means of a Bible or prayer-book placed under my pillow. The first night of our lodging there made an indelible impression on the memory. The place swarmed with rats, by whose persevering efforts large mounds of dirt had been thrown up in the cellar, and from one of its windows to another the grass had been completely worn by their feet. What with the noise they made in running about, the continued and antiphonal barkings of dogs on the one side of the creek to those on the other, and of both, for all I know, to the full moon, (aided also by the voice of our own dog within or near to the house,) the yelling of cats, and the moanings of doves that had made their nests in the eaves of the long one-storied building, it was impossible to sleep with comfort, and equally so not to feel that the house was indeed haunted by natural beings both within and without, who were quite capable of annoying its sleepless inmates. Dinah, our servant-woman, would never stay at home when we were out to tea, unless she had the company and protection of her faithful husband. We found half a year's residence quite enough in this solitary mansion, and afterwards removed to a comfortable dwelling in the town, which we occupied during the remaining time of my connection with the parish.

As soon as I became settled, I made systematic arrangements for ministerial duties, becoming acquainted with all the, members of both parishes. The families, without exception, I regularly visited; those in the town once in about a month or six weeks and some oftener. The country residents were not so easily accessible; but, as I kept a horse and chaise, I rode a good deal, and neglected none, however remote, who attended either of the churches. As I was the only Episcopal clergyman in the county, the length of which was at least forty miles, my time was considerably occupied in going about, especially when sickness prevailed. Still, I found by experience, that habitual regularity and order were great helps to effort. I entered upon my parochial charge with about twenty-five sermons, most of which at that time I ventured to preach, although subsequently I burned the larger portion. Some, however, I have preserved, as they may be suggestive to you, if you take the trouble to read them. I preached in the town church and in St. Paul's alternately every other Sunday morning. After officiating at the town church in the morning, I usually held a second service either there, or, when the season was suitable, at I. U. in the afternoon, or else employed the time in catechetical instruction. During one season this service was conducted for the exclusive benefit of the colored population. On these occasions the lower part of the church was generally quite full. The congregations were always attentive to the instruction which I endeavored to give them clearly and simply; many of them joined audibly and earnestly in the devotions; and, I need not say, they sang "lustily and with a good courage." After performing the morning duty at St. Paul's, I used to officiate also in the afternoon at the town church, except when in winter the roads were too bad to allow me, after a service beginning at eleven, to ride eight miles in time for another service the same day.

Usually I limited my pulpit preparations to one sermon a week, irrespective, however, of occasional calls of duty, such as funerals, when in compliance with long-established usage, sermons were expected. Frequently, a large proportion of the hearers consisted of persons who were not in the habit of attending church, so that in this way an opportunity was given to make known the truth to those who refused to put themselves under the ordinary course of edification. After I had been two months in the parish I established a course of Wednesday evening services. These were continued with some intermissions and changes, during a large proportion of the time that I lived in Chestertown. I began with the first Epistle to the Corinthians. I did not venture to explain the Romans. The first lecture was delivered on the evening of April sixteenth, 1812, and the series was continued until June. In the following November—about which time those persons who had been attacked by ague or intermittent fever during the summer or autumn usually recovered—it was resumed. Occasionally I reserved the consideration of very important texts for Sundays, especially certain portions in the second Epistle. Lectures were delivered also on other subjects, as occasion required, namely, baptism, confirmation, and the Lord's Supper. I also prepared and delivered six lectures on the first part of the Church Catechism, namely, the Christian covenant. I would probably have attempted to illustrate the whole of this "INSTRUCTION" of the Church if I had continued in the parish. It was my invariable practice to begin the preparation of my sermon not later than Tuesday, generally on Monday. I devoted to it about two hours every morning, beginning directly after breakfast, and usually finished on Friday. I never allowed myself to wait until I should get in a humor for writing. Experience satisfied me that this came naturally in the very exercise, (*l'appétit vient en mangeant,*) though it may have been commenced reluctantly and even with aversion. As a general rule, the rest of my mornings, and the evenings which were not spent in visiting my friends, were devoted to study, and the afternoons to parochial visits. Of course this arrangement was subject to many interruptions; but still I found myself able to carry it out in a very considerable degree, and, I think I may add, to advantage.

The chief topics of study to which I bent my attention were the Bible and ecclesiastical history—principally the former. I read a good deal of Hebrew; but, unfortunately, on an erroneous principle—ignoring the points. Some years afterwards I felt the truth of a remark which I heard made in Philadelphia by an earnest advocate of the Divine authority, not only of the Hebrew words and letters, but also of the vowel-points and accents, when he was declaiming against the system of Masclef as not tending to give the learner any clear and solid knowledge of the language: "You may plough a field through, and you may have to plough it through over again." I read the Septuagint through, beginning February eighth, 1814, and finishing it October eleventh, 1815. But I made the great mistake of merely reading it without comparing it with the Hebrew, or any translation —our own good old English, for example. The advantage derived was consequently very doubtful, and the impression made on my mind soon wore off. On June eighth, 1814, I commenced the study of the sacred history of the Old Testament, intending to make use of such works as I could readily procure. Among them Stackhouse's History of the Bible was prominent. In examining the Pentateuch, I availed myself of Jenning's Jewish Antiquities, and Graves' Lectures on its last four books. About the same time, I read also Leusden's Philologus Hebræomixtus, Bishop Lowth on the Sacred Poetry of the Hebrews, Gregory's translation, studying the quotations from the Old Testament in the original, Warburton's Divine Legation of Moses, and various other works bearing on the subject of the Scriptures. At one period I devoted a considerable portion of my time to Latin and Greek

classics.   Between October twenty-third, 1815,
and June, 1818, I read the following works in
Latin : Cicero de Officiis, his Orations, de Ora-
tore, Senectute, Amicitia, Paradoxa ad M. Bru-
tum, Scipionis Somnium, Sallust Bell. Catal.
et Jugurth. twice ; Florus, Cæsar, Comment. de
Bell. Gallico et Civile, A. Hirt. Pansæ Comment.
de Bell. Alexandrino, Afric. and Hisp., Suetonius
de XII. Cæsaribus, Taciti Annales, Historia de
Moribus Germanorum, de Vita Agricolæ, and
Quinctilian de Oratoribus.   During the same period I read in Greek, Longinus on the Sublime
three times, the Oration of Æschines against
Ctesiphon twice, Chrysostom on the Priesthood
twice, Demosthenes on the Crown twice.   On
the twentieth of June, 1816, I undertook to
study the Philippics.   I had nothing to aid
me but the Greek text, and an old and much-
worn edition of Scapula's Lexicon, which I may
say I used laboriously.   By the eighteenth of
September I had read all the eleven Philippics
carefully, the ninth and tenth three times, all
the others four, and two five times.   Philip's
Letter to the Athenians, and the Oration on the
Letter, I read three times.   The only other
Greek classics which were studied at that time
were Lucian's Dialogues, and the Medea and
Alcestis of Euripides.   These were read twice.

I read, also, but not very carefully, the first book of Origen against Celsus. I am still very decidedly of the opinion that habitual repetition is the most effectual process to insure facility in understanding ancient authors. I must express my regret that, in general, our schools and colleges compel their pupils to read so much—suffering them, also, to advance to the highest classes — while, in numerous instances, little or nothing is thoroughly mastered. It is a fundamental mistake, and a main cause of the general want of accurate classical knowledge.

In preparing my sermons, I laid it down as a principle, never to make a positive statement respecting any point of doctrine or fact, unless I thought that I could prove it; or, at least, was quite confident that it could be maintained. Doubtless, like many young preachers, I often did make incorrect statements; but the habit I thereby acquired, of considering how the truth of each proposition might be evinced, made me somewhat cautious, and, no doubt, often led me to correct a hastily-formed opinion, or the statement of an imperfectly known fact. I endeavored, also, to be governed by a rule which I had seen laid down in Claude's *Essay on the Composition of a Sermon,* and which made a strong impression on me in early life: EXPLAIN TERMS. The application of this rule compelled me to consider carefully the meaning of the declarations made, and, I can not but believe, contributed to greater accuracy of statement. Indeed, it is my opinion, which has been strengthened by the observation of every additional year of life, that if writers on divinity had always set this rule before them, and written in accordance with it, the Church would have been saved from the burden of a mass of theological logomachy. We should, doubtless, have had fewer dogmatical and controversial books than now load the shelves of libraries; but those few would be proportionately more accurate and intelligent.

I continued to hold the two parishes thus associated for three years. At the expiration of that period, I relinquished St. Paul's, the Rev. Mr. Handy taking charge of that parish, and confined myself to that of Chestertown. About that time, or a year before, I organized a Sunday-school in connection with the church in town. My sister and some other ladies devoted themselves to the business of instruction. This was among the earliest Sunday-schools established in our Church. Indeed, I do not know of any that preceded it, except that in the parish of Swedesborough, under the care of the Rev. Simon Wilmer. I have reason to believe that it was very useful in the community. I succeeded, also, in founding, in 1816, the Kent County Bible Society, which was very generally patronized. The most decided and high-toned Episcopalians of that vicinity never seemed to think that a union of different Christians, for the purpose of disseminating the sacred Scriptures, could possibly be inconsistent with sound church principles.

When I first settled in Maryland, the Right Reverend Thomas John Claggett, who had been consecrated September seventeenth, 1792, was the diocesan. He appeared to be very much respected and beloved, but in consequence of his age and infirmities it was thought expedient to appoint an assistant, who should also succeed him on his death. At the meeting of the Convention in Baltimore in 1814, when the subject was brought up for consideration, the Bishop did not seem to be favorable to this measure, and therefore, when the question was taken, I gave my vote in the negative. My course gave no slight satisfaction to the party of the Rev. Mr. Dashiell, the rector of St. Peter's Church, Baltimore, who was as conspicuous for the warmth and earnestness of his preaching as he afterwards became for his inconsistent conduct which caused his deposition from the ministry. The majority of the Convention being in favor, however, of having an Assistant Bishop, it was decided to go into an election. Mr. Dashiell endeavored to prevail upon me to vote in such a way as might tend to prevent the election of the Rev. Dr. James Kemp, of Cambridge, Dorchester county, a prominent clergyman whom the leading members of the Convention had resolved to sustain. Although I had voted in opposition to the appointment of any assistant, yet when I found that a majority of the Convention were in favor of the measure, I thought it quite consistent to yield to the general wish, and gave my vote for Dr. Kemp. I afterwards saw a good deal of this gentleman, and accompanied him during some of his visitations in Kent and Queen Anne's counties, and in a portion of the State of Delaware which lay contiguous to Maryland. I found him uniformly kind and amiable. Although he was always classed among what are called the high-church clergy, yet his views were quite liberal, and his practice sufficiently accommodating. I distinctly recollect officiating for him in the church at Shrewsbury, when he directed me to omit the ante-communion service, and preached immediately after I had gone through the morning prayer. Some time after I left the diocese, he had a difficulty with certain of his clergy, but I am not enough acquainted with its nature to give any account of or to express any opinion about it. His memory is deservedly cherished by the Church.

During the war between the United States and Great Britain, which commenced in 1812, the counties lying on the Chesapeake Bay and the rivers emptying into it, were very much annoyed by the enemy. Country places were rifled and destroyed, and villages burned. Among the latter were Georgetown and Frederick, on the Sassafras river, the former in Kent county, and the latter in Cecil, directly opposite, about nineteen miles north-east of Chestertown. The alarm and agitation produced, and the apprehension that this town would soon be subjected to the same fate, induced a large proportion of the inhabitants to remove their most valuable furniture and other property into the country. Happily, however, we escaped the apprehended evil, though not without the occurrence of events fitted to deepen our sense of thankfulness at our exemption.

On the night of the thirtieth of August a party of men under the command of Sir Peter Parker, landed and marched some miles into the interior, to an open space called, from the owner of the farm to which it · belonged, Caulk's field, which was about nine miles from Chester. A small company of militia, gathered from the town and the surrounding county, were encamped in the vicinity, under the command of Col. Philip Reed. Ezekiel F. Chambers, Isaac Spenser, John B. Eccleston, Esqs., and Major and Captain Hickes were among the leading officers. These were all, except one, communicants of my church. The moon was full, and the sky perfectly clear and bright. The Americans had been lying under the shelter of a thick wood, and when they emerged into the open field an engagement took place between the two parties. The Americans had the decided advantage of being, from their practice of shooting canvas-back ducks and other such game, well-trained and skillful marksmen. The conflict was of short duration, and the enemy, although greatly superior in numbers, were soon compelled to quit the field, carrying with them many who were wounded, and leaving one midshipman and eight men dead on the field, besides nine so much injured that six died in the course of a few hours. A contemporary writes :* "Sir Peter Parker of the Menelaus, one of the most distinguished officers of the British navy, was among the slain. He was mortally wounded with a buckshot, and died before reaching the barges, to which he was conveyed by his men. Certain information from the enemy assures us that their total loss in killed and wounded was forty-two or forty-three, including two wounded lieutenants." Perhaps the unnatural excitement of the foe exposed them the more to their cool and deliberate antagonists, the British, it was said, having spent the early part of the night in carousing. It is a very remarkable fact that not a single American lost his life, and only one received a wound, and that not serious. Balls passed through the coats of several, but by the particular providence of God, their persons were preserved from harm. I have been surprised that this engagement excited at the time so little general attention, and has since been scarcely ever noted.

On the announcement of peace there was a

* Letter of Col. Reed to Brig.-Gen. Benjamin Chambers, dated Camp at Belle Aire, third Sept., 1814, published in the Kent *Inquirer* of June thirtieth, 1832, and republished in the Kent *News*, Chestertown, Md., of Feb. seventh, 1857.

general rejoicing. The town was illuminated, and the windows ornamented with appropriate devices. An old inhabitant, an earnest Methodist, William Harris, was particularly gratified by seeing in the window of my house, illuminated portions from Psalms 46 : 9,* 118 : 27,† and one or two other similar texts. From the latter passage of the Psalms I preached on April thirteenth, 1815, that being the day appointed for a general thanksgiving. Of course I did not omit to call the attention of the congregation to the remarkable fact that not an individual had been killed in the various engagements and skirmishes in which they had taken part, and to urge it as a reason for special gratitude to God.

* He maketh wars to cease unto the ends of the earth; he breaketh the bow, and cutteth the spear in sunder; he burneth the chariot in the fire.

† God is the Lord, which hath showed us light: bind the sacrifice with cords, even unto the horns of the altar.

CHAPTER III.

Pernicious Effects of Climate and Slavery—He is offered a Professorship at Annapolis—Leaves Chestertown—Call to Germantown, Pa.—St. Ann's, Brooklyn—Elizabeth, New-Jersey—Rev. Dr. Bowen—Grace Church, New-York—Dr. Jarvis—Return to Philadelphia—Visits Chestertown, Washington, and various places in Virginia, returning by Central Pennsylvania—His Mother's Death—Her Character—Historical and Theological Studies—Labors in Philadelphia—Trinity Church the Result—Preached the Opening Sermon.

DURING the time of my residence in Maryland, most parts of the Eastern Shore were subject to agues and intermittent fevers; and much exposure to the hot sun and the heavy dews of June, July, and August was very likely to produce disease. The long and unvarying continuance also of the warmth of summer tended to enervate the constitution. I often felt the effects of the climate in producing lassitude and weariness. In 1816, I had an attack of intermittent, which for a considerable time incapacitated me for parochial duty, and enfeebled my constitution. As I perceived that the effect of repeated attacks of this sort was to injure the physical system and to induce other diseases not easily re-

3*

moved, I began to entertain serious thoughts of transferring my residence to a more northern and salubrious climate. The pernicious effects also of slavery on habits and energies had considerable influence in ripening my thoughts and feelings into a fixed determination. I could have settled, and in some respects advantageously, at Annapolis. I had an offer of a Latin professorship in the college at one thousand dollars a year, in connection with which position I could have obtained a church in the neighborhood with a salary of six hundred dollars. But I did not choose to accept a position which I should not have been willing to retain. In the summer of 1817 I resigned my charge of the church at Chestertown, which I had held for five years and a half. I preached my farewell sermon on the morning of August tenth, 1817, from Phil. 4 : 7, having commenced the subject suggested by the text on the previous Sunday. I left my parishioners with feelings of sincere regard and affection, which, I have good reason to believe, were very generally reciprocated.

When I resigned the church at Chestertown, I expected to go immediately to Germantown, near Philadelphia, to become pastor of a newly formed congregation in that place. There was

at that time, no church-edifice, but it was expected that arrangements for erecting one
would be carried into effect without delay; and
these expectations were soon afterwards real-
ized. The situation of rector had been offered
to me; but as I delayed for some time to give
a decided answer, some of the leading men became dissatisfied, and they called another candidate, the Rev. Mr. Dupuy of Philadelphia,
who accepted the invitation.

I could not blame the vestry for thus
passing me over, as they might reasonably
have expected a prompt reply, and perhaps
they considered my delay as disrespectful.
The cause of my not immediately accepting the offer will appear from what follows.
Before I was invited to Germantown, my old
friend, Mr. Feltus, who for some years had
been rector of St. Ann's Church, Brooklyn,
L. I., had been called to St. Stephen's, New-
York, to succeed the Rev. Richard Channing
Moore, who had been consecrated Bishop of
the diocese of Virginia. Mr. Feltus, still retaining his former friendship for me, was desirous that I should succeed him. The situation
would have been to me very agreeable. Accordingly, at his solicitation, I made him a visit,
and officiated in his church. He assured me

that there was no doubt of my being chosen; consequently, I expected to receive the call, and therefore delayed for a time my reply to the invitation from Germantown.

On this occasion, however, I fell between two tubs. When I consented to appear as a candidate for St. Ann's, I was not aware that the friends of another clergyman, a young deacon lately ordained, were endeavoring to secure the place for him. He had the decided advantage of being personally known, as he had married the daughter of an influential member of the vestry. I was told, also, that his appointment was strongly favored by the bishop of the diocese. The result was, that he was chosen by a majority of one. Afterward his health became impaired. A Southern climate was thought desirable, and he removed to Augusta, in Georgia. Subsequently, he came to the North, and settled first in Hartford, Connecticut, afterwards in the Mission Church in Vandewater street, New-York, and lastly, as rector of St. Peter's Church, where he died, generally esteemed and beloved. I refer to my respected friend, the Rev. Dr. Hugh Smith.

Thus I failed to get the parish of my old acquaintance and adviser, and lost, I may say, that of Germantown. But all these matters are subject to the working of Providence, whose agency gradually discloses itself out of the dark recesses of human error and disappointment. Before I left Chestertown, it was suggested to me by a friend, who was one of the vestry, to withdraw my resignation. But I could not consent to do this, as my reason for desiring a more northern residence still remained in full force. I therefore sold my furniture and returned to my father's. I had not been there more than two or three weeks, when I received a request to supply the place of the Rev. Dr. Rudd, of Elizabethtown, New-Jersey, who wished to go to Ohio, and other parts of the Western country, and expected to be absent two or three months. As my expenses were to be paid, and I had no particular employment in view, and was informed, also, that the society was agreeable and the town pleasant, and as it was in the vicinity of New-York, where my sister, Mrs. Warner, and her daughter resided, I complied with the request, and removed to Elizabethtown. There I spent ten weeks most agreeably, and, I hope, somewhat usefully. I officiated twice every Sunday, and had evening lectures during the week. Six of these were on the Communion Service. The course was imperfect, as the rector returned before I had time to complete it. The acquaintances I formed there were exceedingly kind and friendly; several were highly intelligent, and some ranked among the most respectable families in the State. On my leaving them, at the return of Dr. Rudd, the ladies of the congregation presented me with a handsome gown and cloth cloak, together with some bands and cambric pocket-handkerchiefs. The donation was accompanied by a very kind and courteous note, to which I need hardly add that I replied as my feelings dictated, and in such terms as the sincere respect, which I cherished for them, naturally prompted.

As the proximity of Elizabethtown to New-York led me to make occasional visits to the city, I became the better acquainted with some of the clergy whom I had known slightly before. One of the most distinguished for intelligence, gentlemanly bearing, and Christian character, was the Rev. Nathaniel Bowen, D.D., rector of Grace Church. The death of that most estimable and devoted man, Bishop Dehon, having left the Diocese of South-Carolina vacant, Dr. Bowen was chosen to succeed him. Before determining whether to accept the appointment or not, he was desirous of making a visit to the diocese. Soon after my engagement at Elizabethtown had expired, he proposed to me to supply his place in Grace Church, during the winter, that he might make his contemplated visit. I feared to undertake so responsible a charge. My health was not very good, as the influence of the climate of Kent county had not been favorable to my constitution, and my residence in the flat region of Elizabethtown had not invigorated it. In order to diminish the amount of duty, the rector proposed that I should officiate in the mornings, intending to secure the services of Dr. Jarvis, then rector of St. Michael's, Bloomingdale, for the afternoons. I consented to this arrangement, and the month of December found me residing in New-York, and filling as well as I could, the position of the rector of Grace Church. As Dr. Jarvis took the afternoon service, I became intimately acquainted with him.

My temporary connection with Grace Church was the occasion of my forming friendships with some most estimable persons, with whom I should otherwise have had nothing more than a passing acquaintance I became somewhat intimate with the celebrated jurist, David B. Ogden; also with the distinguished John Wells, with whose eldest son and daughters I have had the satisfaction of cultivating a warm friendship during a long course of years. I formed an intimacy, also, with the family of Mr. Isaac Lawrence, and received from them a continued succession of kindnesses, and with John Pintard, one of the warmest-hearted and most generous of men. These friendships lasted till death dissolved the earthly tie, and thus prepared the way, as I trust, for a closer connection hereafter.

In April, 1818, I returned to Philadelphia. My health had not been firm during the winter, and, as spring advanced, I resolved to take the advice of the family, and make a journey on horseback. I procured, therefore, a very pleasant little horse, and some time in June set out on my excursion. I bent my course first to Chestertown, where I made a very agreeable visit among my old friends and parishioners. Crossing the Chesapeake in a packet from Rock Hall, steamers not being then in use, I went to Baltimore. From there I rode to Annapolis, Georgetown, Washington, and then to Alexandria, to see my former friend, Dr. William Wilmer. He took me to Mount Vernon, where I had the gratification, though not unmingled with melancholy, of visiting Washington's tomb, so little worthy of such a man, and of going through his residence. Afterwards I directed my course westward in Loudon county, along the Potomac, to Harper's Ferry. In consequence of abundant rains, I got but an imperfect view of the magnificent scenery. Leaving this point, I went to Hancock. As there was no regular ferry at this place, I crossed the river in a small boat, my horse swimming by the side of it. A ride of eight miles brought me to Bath, a beautiful spot, frequented in the summer by gentry from the vicinity, for health and pleasure. As the season was not sufficiently advanced for company, I found myself alone in the spacious mansion. The next day I returned to Hancock, and, crossing Sideling Hill and other mountainous elevations, where, for miles, I saw scarcely a solitary house, I journeyed on to Bedford Springs. After riding some distance along the Juniata river, I returned home by the way of Carlisle, Harrisburgh, and Lancaster, having been absent about six weeks. During all this time, I met with only one accident. One day, on a turnpike near the Juniata, my attention was attracted by a man lying in a state of intoxication on the side of the road. Thinking he might be ill, I rode hastily across, and as I was bending on one side to look at him the more closely, my horse shied, and threw me on the hard ground. Running off immediately, he dragged me a short distance, till, my shoe being pulled off, I was left lying on the road. Fortunately, I had not for some time been accustomed to wear boots, and made the whole journey with shoes; otherwise, I might have been severely injured. I was somewhat bruised, but soon arose and went after my horse, which had been stopped at a neighboring toll-gate.

On arriving at Philadelphia, I was met near my father's house by a man whom I had occasionally seen before, as he lived in the neighborhood. He accosted me in the words: "Well, you have heard the news, I suppose?" On inquiring what he meant, he shocked me with the intelligence that my mother had died suddenly the day before. Arriving at the house, I found my father and sisters in deep distress. However greatly I lamented my absence on occasion of this bereavement, I could not but feel thankful that I had been permitted to return home in health, and in time enough to see my dear mother's remains consigned to the tomb. She had lived to a good old age, having passed the period of three-score years and ten, greatly respected and beloved by all who

knew her. Without the least intention of
writing her eulogy, I must say that she was a
sincerely pious, humble Christian woman, and
attached to the Episcopal Church of her fathers, in which she had been educated, and
had always continued a devoted member.
Her life was governed by a conscientious sense
of duty. In her domestic relations, she combined kindness with energy, and was noted
for habitual attention to all family duties.
She was indefatigable in her endeavors to promote the interests and wishes of those with
whom she had formed friendships. As a
neighbor, she was always disposed to assist
any who might need offices of kindness; and
especially the poor, who were in the habit of
soliciting advice and help in cases of sickness.
Her knowledge of the nature of some diseases,
and the character and action of certain medi-
cines, which was obtained probably from her
father, peculiarly fitted her for this. Some
years before her death, she had suffered severely from a paralytic attack, from which
she gradually recovered. A second succeeded
it; and the third, which most probably was
also apoplectic, carried her off suddenly. Her
death took place on the seventeenth day of
June, 1818. A letter, apprising me of her ill-

ness, had been sent to Lancaster, but I had left there before it arrived.

I now settled myself at the old paternal mansion, reading history, and pursuing theological studies. In the autumn, or early in the winter, I established a Sunday-night lecture at a school-room opposite our house, and gathered together a small congregation. Subsequently a large room was secured in a public building two streets below, which was known by the name of the Commissioners' Hall. The Rev. William Richmond, originally of Providence, Rhode Island, who had been a candidate for the ministry in the city of New-York, and lately admitted to deacons' orders, was invited to take charge of the congregation. He became very intimate with my father, who conceived a strong attachment to him. Efforts were soon made to build a church. The site selected was on Catherine street, directly opposite our vegetable-garden. Three lots were obtained, and subscriptions taken to raise the necessary funds. My father gave one thousand dollars; and my sisters, with the aid of a few friends, established what was called a Mite Society, which collected at various times, in small sums, the amount of three thousand dollars. A neat and comfortable brick building was put up, at the cost of seven thousand dollars. My father, however, did not live to see the completion of Trinity Church, that being the name by which it was called, in accordance with his wish. I had been then residing in New-York for some time, but being requested by Bishop White, who knew the interest that our family had taken in the church, and the efforts made by them to secure its permanent establishment, to deliver the opening sermon, I was present at its consecration. This took place on the morning of January seventeenth, 1822, when I preached from Psalm 95 : 6, on the subject of public worship. Mr. Richmond having already accepted a call to St. Michael's, Bloomingdale, New-York, the vestry invited the Rev. Manning Brinkly Roche to take charge of the parish. He remained, however, but a short time, and was succeeded by the Rev. Levi Silliman Ives, who afterwards made himself so noted by apostatizing to Rome, after having exercised for several years the office of Bishop in North-Carolina. By this act he disclosed theological views at utter variance with those held by him while rector of Trinity Church. After him, the Rev. William C. Mead, now rector of the church in Norwalk, Connecticut, became the pastor, and the Rev. Mr. Coleman succeeded him.

CHAPTER IV.

Appointed Superintendent of the Theological School in Phila-
delphia—Bishop Alonzo Potter his first Pupil—Translation of
"Bochart's Phaleg"—A General Theological Seminary Proposed in the General Convention—Measures Taken for its Establishment—History of its Formation and Organization—
Mr. Turner Elected Professor of "Historic Theology" —
Charged Temporarily with the Duties of the Professor of Systematic Theology—Dr. C. C. Moore's Gift to the Seminary—
Rev. Dr. Gadsden's "Statement for the Seminary"—South-
Carolina its Originator—The Error of the Bishop of Oxford in
ascribing it to the Influence of Bishop Hobart—First Students in the Seminary—Professor Turner's Course of Instruction.

In the latter part of the year 1818, the
Society for the Advancement of Christianity
in Pennsylvania, appropriated a sum of money,
to a "clergyman, whose duty it should be to act
as a teacher of theology, provided the ecclesiastical authority of the State (diocese) should
make such appointment."* The authority referred to was no doubt the Bishop of the diocese, acting probably in connection with the
standing committee; and it conferred on me the
appointment of "Superintendent of Theological

* Seventh Annual Report, read at St. James's Church, January sixth,
1819.

Students." The salary was merely nominal, only one hundred and fifty dollars a year. My duty was to direct their studies, and hear them recite. The arrangement lasted but a very short time, being superseded by another of a more definite and permanent character. Only two candidates attended me regularly. One of them was Mr. Samuel Sitgreaves, of Easton, Pennsylvania, a nephew of the Rev. Mr. (now Bishop) Kemper, who at that time was one of the assistant ministers of the three united churches of which Bishop White was rector. Mr. Sitgreaves died not many years afterwards. The other student was Alonzo Potter, who has since made himself so eminent as a man and a scholar, and who now fills the office of Bishop in the diocese of Pennsylvania, with so much honor to himself, usefulness to the Church, and benefit to the cause of learning and religion. When a student he gave evidence of that quickness and accuracy of perception, that varied and extensive information, that sound and discriminating mind, for which he has been distinguished through life. When he entered upon the study of divinity, he had not received baptism. On occasion of his public admission by this holy sacrament into the church of Christ, which took place in St. Peter's, Philadelphia, the Bishop officiating, I was his witness. Ever since that period, I have had the satisfaction of an intimate acquaintance with my first pupil, to whom I felt at the time, that I was not competent to give such instruction as was adapted to his intellectual ability.

During my previous residence at Elizabeth-town and New-York, I had employed a good deal of my leisure time on a translation into English of Bochart's Phaleg. This is the first part of his *Geographia Sacra*. After examining in the first book, various topics suggested by a comparison of facts and statements in Genesis with correspondences, real or supposed, which are contained in classical and oriental antiquity, the author, in the three following, draws from the same ancient sources all that can be found relating respectively to the posterity of Shem, Japhet and Ham. The second part, which is in two books, occupies about as much space as the four of the former, and treats of the colonies and language of the Phœnicians. I had begun the translation some years before, intending to go through both parts. This work, which seems to have exhausted all the ancient sources of information, on the geographical, historical, and philological points of which it treats, was made known to me by Dr. Wylie,

while I was pursuing with him the study of
Hebrew, and I examined a good deal of it
with much interest. Along with it I read
Gale's *Court of the Gentiles*, a very curious and
learned production, which the Doctor lent me,
the author of which borrowed largely from
Bochart. I for a long time cherished the idea
that a translation of this work would be highly acceptable to literary people, and particularly to the clergy, who would eagerly seize
the opportunity of making themselves acquainted with its ancient treasures, and of
confirming thereby their faith in the statements of the Old Testament Scriptures, especially of the Book of Genesis. Under this
impression, I worked assiduously until I had
got into the third book, when my enthusiasm
cooled very much, and I brought my trans-
lating labors to a close. The numerous quotations from Latin and Greek writers I left
untranslated, which was a great mistake, as the
English reader would have required a version
of those, as well as of the author's language.
After abandoning the undertaking, I never attempted to revise the translation, and have
scarcely looked at the manuscript since. The
profoundly learned work remains in its original dress, for students who can read Latin, and

4

are willing to take some trouble in order to acquire such antiquarian lore as tends to elucidate and confirm the word of God.

The subject of a Theological Seminary, for the benefit of candidates for the ministry, had for some years past engaged the attention of some of the most prominent bishops and clergy of the Episcopal Church. Such institutions were already in existence in several other denominations, some of them in active operation, and one at least—that of Andover, Massachusetts —largely endowed and flourishing. The matter was brought for consideration before the General Convention held in the city of New-York in May, 1817. On the twenty-sixth, the House of Bishops adopted the following resolutions, which had been drawn up by Bishop Dehon :*

"*Resolved*, That it is expedient to establish, for the better education of the candidates for holy orders in this Church, a General Theological Seminary, which may have the united support of the whole Church in these United States, and be under the superintendence and control of the General Convention.

"*Resolved*, That this Seminary be located in the city of New-York.

* See Dr. Gadsden's Statement made in the Convention of South-Carolina, February nineteenth, 1819.

"*Resolved*, That —— persons be appointed by the House of Bishops to visit the several parts of the United States, and solicit contributions towards funds for founding and endowing such an institution.

"*Resolved*, That a Committee be appointed, to consist of the presiding Bishop, and the Bishops of this Church in New-York and New-Jersey, with three clergymen and three laymen, to be appointed by the House of Clerical and Lay Deputies; which Committee shall be empowered to receive and manage such funds as shall be collected—to devise a plan for establishing and carrying into operation such an institution; which plan shall be communicated to the several Bishops of this Church; and in the event of sufficient funds being obtained, if a majority of the Bishops shall have approved the plan, to carry it into immediate operation."

"These resolutions were concurred in by the House of Clerical and Lay Deputies; and they appointed as a Committee on their part, the following gentlemen, namely:

"*Of the Clergy*—The Rev. Dr. WHARTON, the Rev. Dr. How, the Rev. Dr. HARRIS.

"*Of the Laity*—Hon. RUFUS KING, WILLIAM MEREDITH, Esq., Hon. CHARLES F. MERCER."

In accordance with one of the resolutions,
"the Rev. Daniel Burhans, of Newtown, Connecticut, the Rev. Nathaniel Bowen, D.D., of
the city of New-York, and the Rev. William
H. Wilmer, of Alexandria," were appointed
to solicit contributions in different States for
the proposed institution. Each of these gentlemen was furnished with the necessary papers, certified by the presiding Bishop, who
also accompanied them with a lucid exposition
of his own views and those of his Episcopal
brethren, on the great importance and usefulness of a proper theological training for the
ministry, and the advantages which might reasonably be expected to result from the establishment of a Seminary for the purpose.

In the month of October, of the same year,
Bishop Hobart addressed the Convention of
the State of New-York on the same subject.
He began by the statement that "without a
ministry, the Church can not *exist;* and destitute of a *learned* as well as a *pious* ministry,
she can not *flourish.*" He then proceeded to
show the vast importance of establishing the
proposed divinity-school, and urged the duty
of making liberal ·contributions, in order to
carry the design into vigorous effect.

On the twelfth of December, Bishop White,

as Chairman of the Theological Committee
appointed by the General Convention, increased the number of persons to collect contributions by adding twenty-five names of gentlemen resident in the city of New-York, seven
of whom were clergymen. This was done in
accordance with the wish of Dr. Bowen, and
at the representation of New-York members.

On the fifteenth and sixteenth of January,
1818, the Committee held a meeting in Philadelphia, and adopted certain resolutions bearing on the subject. They also addressed a
letter "to the Members of the Protestant
Episcopal Church in the United States," showing the importance and necessity of establishing such an institution. It was signed by
Bishops White, Hobart, and Croes; also by
Dr. Wharton and Mr. Meredith. The Rev.
Dr. Harris, then President of Columbia College, and the Hon. Mr. Mercer, of Virginia,
"members of the Committee unavoidably pre-
vented from attendance," expressed their approbation of the address.

The next meeting of the Committee was
held in the same city on the seventh and
eighth of October, in the same year, the same
gentlemen also being present as before. Eight
resolutions were then passed, "the first being

proposed by Bishop White, and the others by Bishop Hobart." The first resolution relates to the establishment of professorships; namely, one of " Biblical Learning," another of "Systematic Theology," a third of " Historic Theology, embracing a view of the Constitution of the Christian Church, of the Orders of the Ministry, and of the Nature and Duty of Christian Unity." The only other professorship was that of " the Ritual of the Church and of Pulpit Eloquence," comprehending " the duties of the Clerical Office." The arrangement was very judicious, and quite worthy of its author.

Of the other resolutions, the fifth was certainly objectionable. It required the professors to " conduct the students through all the books prescribed in the course of study set forth by the House of Bishops, making them thoroughly acquainted with the subjects of which those books respectively treat." Every one who knows what that course is, knows also the impossibility of complying with such a requisition. The limited period even of three years, (and at that time the term of candidateship did not exceed one,) would not allow half the time necessary to study the books referred to. I need not hesitate to say that, at present, no one recommends such a course, and no candidate thinks of attempting such an enterprise. The author of the resolution could not have properly considered what an immense task it imposed.

Among these resolutions was also the following: "That, when the funds of the Institution admit, the Rev. Charles H. Wharton, D.D., be appointed Professor of Systematic Theology, and that the Rev. Samuel F. Jarvis be now appointed Professor of Biblical Learning, and the Rev. Samuel H. Turner Professor of Historic Theology; and that these two last-named Professors receive for the present, and until they can be detached from parochial cares and devoted solely to the objects of the Institution, a salary of eight hundred dollars per annum. That, until the other Professorship be filled, and the Professor of Systematic Theology enter on the duties of his office, the subject of Systematic Theology be assigned to the Professor of Historic Theology, and that the Professors of Biblical Learning and of Historic Theology provide, by joint arrangement, for the object assigned to the Professor of the Ritual of the Church and of Pulpit Eloquence." Inasmuch as the Committee had been constituted by the General Convention with power "to carry the plan into immediate operation, if approved by a majority of the Bishops," I may date my appointment as Professor in the General Theological Seminary from the eighth of October, 1818.*

When the resolutions just stated were announced to me by my friend, the Rev. Jackson Kemper, now Bishop, I shrank at the idea of assuming such a responsibility. The department of Historic Theology alone appeared more than enough for a person of my comparative youth and inexperience as an instructor, and I freely expressed to him my reluctance to undertake the additional duties involved in the resolutions. Mr. Jarvis also felt that it would be difficult, not to say impracticable, to perform the various duties of a parish a few miles from the city, in addition to those of so important a Professorship. These views he expressed to Bishop Hobart, who replied that measures must be taken to release him at once from parochial

---

* The importance and usefulness of a school for the regular training and instruction of candidates for the ministry impressed themselves strongly on my mind before I was ordained. I distinctly recollect that, when I was a student, as early as 1810, I heard a sermon preached in St. Paul's Church by the Rev. Richard Channing Moore, afterwards Bishop of Virginia, which brought the subject very vividly before my mind, and made me think what a blessing it would be to have any direct agency in carrying such an object into effect. The point of association in the sermon which suggested the thought I do not remember.

cares. Whether it was these difficulties or certain others which the Committee refer to, whereby they were induced to alter their arrangements, I do not positively know. In the report to the Convention they remark as follows:

" The plan contemplated in the above resolutions not succeeding, another meeting of the Committee was held in the city of Philadelphia on the seventh of February, 1819, the same persons being present as at the previous meeting." On this occasion Mr. (now Dr.) Clement C. Moore's offer of sixty lots on condition of having erected thereon " the buildings of the Theological School," was made and accepted. The Committee then " assigned to the Professor of Biblical Learning the subjects of Systematic Divinity, and of the Ritual of the Church and Pulpit Eloquence." They passed also this resolution: " That, in consideration of the more extensive sphere of duty assigned to the Professor of Biblical Learning, and of his situation as having a family, his salary be fixed at two thousand five hundred dollars per annum, with a house as soon as one can be erected; and, in the mean time, with an allowance of five hundred dollars per annum in lieu of a house, in the expectation of his applying himself solely to the discharge of the duties of his station;

4*

and that, the same considerations not applying to the Professor of Historic Theology, his salary be fixed at a thousand dollars per annum, in the hope that the funds of the Institution will speedily admit of a more adequate remuneration." Thus I became relieved from the accumulation of responsibility and duty before referred to, and which I was reluctant to undertake. It was imposed on my colleague with a salary sufficiently ample to compensate for any additional labor to which he might be subjected.

At the meeting of the Convention of South-Carolina in 1819, the Rev. Dr. Gadsden, afterwards Bishop of the Diocese, made, on the nineteenth of February, "a statement for the Theological Seminary," which was published by order of the Convention. This able and interesting address shows the great importance of theological knowledge among the clergy, and urges, with the author's characteristic zeal and eloquence, the duty of the Episcopal Church to take measures for increasing and educating its future ministry. Among other things, he makes this statement, which ought ever to be held in view: "The honor of originating the measure for the proposed Seminary belongs to this diocese. It was introduced by our delegates to the General Convention in 1814, and by that body referred to the consideration of the respective dioceses. It was renewed by our delegates in the Convention of 1817, and was then unanimously adopted. We are pledged not to permit this Institution to die in its birth, and to foster it with unceasing care and liberality. May I not be permitted to add that our perseverance is due to the memory of our late Bishop [Dr. Dehon]? In this cause he labored unto death. The resolutions adopted by the General Convention were from his pen." The resolutions in favor of the Seminary which immediately followed the address were unanimously adopted, and the Church in South. Carolina responded to the call of her devoted minister, and contributed nobly to the support of the great object which had occupied his mind, filled his heart, and inspired him with energy and eloquence.*

Early in the spring of 1819, Dr. Jarvis and

* The Bishop of Oxford, in his History of the Protestant Episcopal Church in America, affirms that "it was mainly to Bishop Hobart that this Institution, so full of promise for America, owed its origin." But this statement is not sustained by satisfactory evidence. Dr. Wilberforce's acquaintance with the history of the Seminary seems very imperfect, and his account to have been drawn from very limited sources. He does not even mention the name of Bishop Dehon. See Stanford and Swords' Edition, 1840, chap. xi. p. 263.

I entered upon our duties. Nothing was done to bring the Institution before the Church. No publication was made of its opening, and no inaugural address delivered, or public religious service of any sort performed. Those who might have been expected to make arrangements of this sort relied, perhaps, upon the New-York authorities, who remained ineffective. The number of students was limited to six, constituting one class. Their names are as follows: Lawson Carter, James P. F. Clarke, George Washington Doane, Benjamin Dorr, Manton Eastburn, and William Hinckley Mitchell. With the exception of the last, who died in the spring of 1836, in South-Carolina, where he exercised his ministry, all are still living, and some have become distinguished in the Church. I began my course of instruction in Ecclesiastical History with the Old Testament, using the English Bible, and illustrating from various authorities. Prideaux's Connection was soon adopted as a text-book. In the history of the Christian Church we made use of Mosheim. I endeavored to supply the deficiencies of this manual, and to correct certain of its erroneous views, especially on the subject of the government of the early Church, by introducing additional matters from other sources, and especially the early Church writers themselves. I made considerable use also of his Commentarii de rebus Christianorum ante Constantinum Magnum, and Dissertationes ad Ecclesiasticam Historiam pertinentes. The arrangement of his work I altered, so as to give the student a consecutive view of the facts narrated, and of the doctrines, heresies, usages, and discipline developed in the progress of the history. During the preceding winter I had become very well acquainted with Prideaux and Mosheim, having made a complete abstract of both, with matter selected from other authors. My familiarity with these text-books made the use of a volume in examining a student almost unnecessary.

CHAPTER V.

Indifference of Bishop Hobart and leading New-York Clergymen to the Seminary—Proof of Want of Interest—Difficulties with Professor Jarvis—Professor Turner's Views on certain points of Theology not in Harmony with those of Bishop Hobart—The Seminary removed to New-Haven—Bishop Brownell's Remarks in regard to it—The Seminary organized on a New Plan—Open to Students of all Religious Denominations—Incidents of the Summer's Vacation—Introductory Discourse at New-Haven—Varied and Pleasant Duties in the Seminary—Its Patron's and Friends—His Father's Death—Sketch of his Life.

The General Theological Seminary, as originally established, did not flourish in New-York. It is certain that the leading men in the Church there, did not take much interest in it.* For causes which can only be ascertained from data well known to persons concerned, Bishop Hobart treated it with comparative indifference; and it is not to be questioned that,

* Even after residing in the city some time, as professor, I was asked by Episcopalians of station and character, who supposed that I was on a visit there, how long I intended to remain!

with the great proportion of Churchmen in his diocese, his word and practice were equivalent to law. The place assigned to the Professors for meeting the students was a small room, immediately beyond the corner of the north gallery in St. Paul's Church. Here we attended them daily, both before the summer vacation, and also after it, until the approach of cold weather compelled us to seek a situation where we could enjoy a fire, there being neither chimney nor stove in the room referred to. Accordingly we removed to St. John's, where, sometimes in the vestry-room, which lay then contiguous to the chancel, at the north-east corner of the building, and sometimes in the adjoining part of the church which contained one of the stoves, we continued our attendance on the class. As the church was frequently opened for prayers, and was also in a retired part of the city, it seemed to be the most suitable place which could be selected. After some time, however, we learned that objections had been made to its being used for this purpose; and on one occasion, finding the doors locked, and not being able to enter the church, we were told by the sexton, Mr. Wunenberg, a German, that we could not be allowed to continue there, unless Dr.

Jarvis and myself would supply the fuel. Who authorized the sexton to say so, I do not know, as he gave us no further information. But it is not probable that he would have presumed to make such a communication without some authoritative direction. As we did not choose to comply with this condition, St. John's Church was abandoned. Mr. Carter, one of the students, who at that time was principal of a young ladies' school, kept in the second story of a house on the north-west corner of Broadway and Cedar street, very kindly offered us the use of this room in the afternoon. We gratefully accepted the offer, and there all the exercises of the General Theological Seminary of the Protestant Episcopal Church in the United States of America, were held during the latter months of 1819 and the earlier ones of 1820. I well remember hearing, in that room, Mr. (afterwards Bishop) Doane read, in Greek, portions of the Epistles of Ignatius. The volume used was the edition of Vossius, owned by me, but now the property of the Seminary Library. During the period referred to, I do not remember ever to have been asked where the exercises of the Seminary were conducted. It appeared to me that scarcely any one either knew or cared. And nothing was ever said or done, by those who possessed the right of giving directions, respecting any public opening of the Institution by an address or otherwise, or any examination of the students at the end of a term.

I have said that but little interest was taken in the Seminary during the time of its continuance in New-York. Certain friends of Dr. Jarvis had for some time been desirous of securing his ministerial services in Boston. It was a remarkable coïncidence, that "the same mail which conveyed to him an unofficial account of his appointment" to a professorship, with a salary of eight hundred dollars, brought also the intelligence that the vestry of Trinity Church, Boston, were about to appoint him assistant minister of that church. And soon after he had official notice of his appointment as professor, he "received also a copy of the vote of the vestry, together with a unanimous vote of the congregation, approving of their proceedings." Thus the offer of the two positions was contemporaneous. At first the Doctor felt strongly inclined to accept that of Trinity Parish in preference to the professorship, but when the arrangement was made which enabled him to dissolve his connection with his church in Bloomingdale, and devote

himself exclusively to the duties of his professorship, he decided in favor of the latter position, and accepted it on March sixth, 1819.
But within the very short period of two
months after commencing his duties, he came
to the conclusion that no hopes were to be
entertained of the success of the Seminary.
His friends in Boston had already been making
efforts to raise money, in order to build a
church, in the hope that he might be induced
to become its rector, and early in May he gave
a verbal promise to that effect, and on the first
Monday in June informed Bishop Hobart of
his intention.

By some the Seminary's want of success was
attributed to the Doctor's determination to dissolve his connection with it. Its abandonment
by its learned professor was said to account for
the coldness shown to the Institution, and its
very considerable failure. Thus the responsibility of its low state was thrown upon him.
But on the other hand, Dr. Jarvis always maintained that the evident want of interest in the
Seminary determined him to consider favorably the proposition to remove to Boston, and
finally induced him to accept the offer of a
church there. He saw no probability of the
Institution rising to any distinction, and felt

himself authorized to accept what he regarded as a more useful and eligible position.

It is not necessary, neither would it be expedient for me, to enter into any details respecting the difficulties which grew out of this matter. It is enough to say, that the Board of Directors thought it right to reduce Dr. Jarvis's salary to the rate of two thousand dollars a year for the time already spent in connection with the Seminary. They even accorded to him their permission to leave it as soon as he might think proper. The Doctor, however, continued to maintain his position, and also his claim to the stipulated three thousand dollars. He prepared a particular and detailed statement of the whole matter, to be laid, if necessary, before the Committee on the Theological Seminary, appointed by the General Convention which was held in May, 1820, in Philadelphia. Although he was not a member of that Convention, he was present at its meetings. Still he withheld the paper for reasons which I am not able to state.*

Eventually Dr. Jarvis obtained the entire

---

* Some particulars above mentioned I have drawn from that document, for the use of which I am indebted to the author's son, the Rev. S. F. Jarvis, of Thomsonville, Connecticut, who courteously granted me the loan of it. I shall have occasion to resort to it again; and, as before, shall occasionally introduce the very words of the statement.

sum. The Trustees, who met at New-Haven in September, after the removal of the Seminary to that city, passed a resolution recognizing his right to the whole amount. They had been told however at the same time, that nothing more than such a recognition by that body was desired; and that the one thousand dollars which remained unpaid would not be demanded. The Rev. Jackson Kemper, who was present on that occasion, and stood alone in opposing the measure, told me that such a statement had been made to the Board by one of the Doctor's Boston friends. Whether such promise was made by authority I do not know; but this I do know, that Mr. Charles Dennison, the treasurer, informed me that, before leaving New-Haven, Dr. Jarvis applied to him for the money, and that he paid it. I have repeatedly heard that the Doctor applied the money to the support of a young man who afterwards became a student of divinity.

It always appeared to me that the want of interest in the Seminary, while originally in New-York, was not owing to Dr. Jarvis's arrangements to leave it. He uniformly maintained that, on the contrary, this determination of his resulted from the previously manifested indifference. His mind, which before vacil-

lated between the two offers, and was only induced to accept the professorship in consequence of the change of terms and conditions
from those of the original arrangement, became
decided in favor of its first impression, and
thus he resolved to leave the Seminary. Still
I can not but say that his determination was
too hastily formed. He accepted the professorship on the sixth of March. On the twelfth
of the same month a subscription-paper was
prepared in Boston, with the view of raising
the necessary funds to build him a church;
and of this he was informed on the twenty-
fourth. In "the latter part of April, or beginning of May, Mr. Sullivan came to New-
York," and before he left, "on the sixth of
May," Dr. Jarvis had "given him the assurance that he would accept the rectorship of
the church when it should be duly offered."
Thus it appears that, at so early a period, he
had made up his mind that the Institution
would not succeed; and this could not have
been more than six weeks after its opening.
It may well be doubted whether he had allowed time enough to enable him to form such
a conclusion; and whether, after accepting a
position with a salary of three thousand dollars a year, which had been offered with the

express view of removing objections that he had made to the previous arrangement, it was right and proper, in so short a time, to determine on relinquishing it. Still I am confident that delay would have made no change with respect to efforts for the permanent establishment and growth of the Seminary. I do not think that Bishop Hobart was sufficiently satisfied with either him or myself to feel much inclination to encourage the Institution, while we were its only professors. The Bishop was desirous of establishing two courses of study—an imperfect one of a year, and another more complete and extending to the term of three years. Neither of us had any sympathy with his wishes in this respect. Dr. Jarvis had for several years been regarded as a superior biblical scholar, and he directed the attention of the students to the Hebrew and Greek Scriptures. The Bishop was not much versed in that kind of learning, and had no great respect for it. I recollect on one occasion, when I dined at his house, in company with all the students, soon after the reörganization of the Seminary in New-York, referring to the authority of Bishop Marsh of Peterborough, the translator of Michaelis's Introduction, the Bishop set aside his Right Rev. Lordship's authority with the remark: "Oh! he's nothing but a biblical critic!" The acquirements of Dr. Jarvis in this department did not raise him very high in Bishop Hobart's estimation.

My own views on certain points of theology were not in harmony with those of the Bishop. I was also accustomed to express myself with a good degree of honest freedom; and sometimes, no doubt, I was not sufficiently discreet or accurate. On the subject of regeneration I had frequent conversations with him. I never could acquiesce in his opinion on this subject. He limited the idea of regeneration to the merely outward change of a visible covenant relation with God, effected through water baptism. He has been grossly misunderstood, I may say, indeed, misrepresented, as if he did not admit the necessity of an internal change. He certainly did avow it in the plainest possible language, although he expressed this by other words, limiting the application of the term regeneration as I have just stated. On the subject of Episcopacy too, while I agreed with him in the fundamental principle of its being a divine institution, I could not affirm its necessity to the very being of a Church. My views on this point were expressed in the introductory discourse delivered at the opening of the Seminary, on its subsequent removal to New-Haven. I will here quote the passage, which, I learned, was satisfactory to the Churchmen of Connecticut: "The form of government which Jesus Christ or His Apostles may have settled for His body, the Church, and the character and grade of those officers that were appointed for the purpose of administering the word and sacraments, which are the ordinary channels of divine grace, can not be uninteresting subjects to the Christian inquirer. But it must be acknowledged that, in the present day, they do not receive that share of attention which their importance merits. The student of divinity must give them a fair investigation. When this is done, I do not hesitate to express the opinion that the result will be a firm conviction of the apostolic and divine origin of those orders of bishops, priests, and deacons which the Preface to our Ordination Service declares to have been in Christ's Church from the Apostles' time; asserting also that this 'is evident to all men, *diligently* reading holy Scripture and ancient authors.' The establishment of these orders by the Apostles, and the influence of the Holy Spirit in their establishment, are facts which we think very susceptible of proof. With regard to the consequences that may be conceived to be the legitimate conclusions deducible from those facts, agreement in opinion among Churchmen ought not to be demanded, and can not reasonably be expected." (Pages 29, 30.)

I had formed these opinions as the result of a somewhat extensive course of reading on the subject while under the direction of Bishop White, and I have not yet seen reason to alter them. Bishop Hobart, like all Churchmen of similar views with whom I have ever happened to converse on the subject, assumed that, if Episcopacy was of divine origin, it must necessarily be permanent; whereas this is the very point to be proved. The same principle, applied to the doctrine of ecclesiastical parity, was assumed by Cartwright and other Puritans, and is examined and refuted by Hooker.* At one time, in arguing with the Bishop, I referred to Bishop White, and also to Hooker. In reply, he alluded to the pamphlet which the Bishop published in August, 1782, entitled, "The Case of the Episcopal Churches Considered."† Here he advocates the appointment of some presbyters as superintendents, with the

---

* Book iii. sec. 10, vol. i. p. 394, *et seq.* Oxford edition of 1793.

† Some notice of this publication may be seen in Dr. Wilson's *Memoir of the Life of Bishop White*, p. 81, *et seq.*

power of ordination; such authority, however, to last no longer than the existing emergency which, he maintains, made it then necessary. Bishop Hobart's language to me was in these very words, "He wanted to make Presbyterians of us all;" to which he added: "Bishop White's inconsistency — and Hooker's inconsistency, too, if you will." I did not believe, and never have believed, that either of these distinguished men was chargeable with inconsistency on the point in question. My only motive in mentioning these circumstances is to show how improbable it is that Bishop Hobart could regard with much interest and satisfaction a Seminary under the instruction of two professors, between whose theological preferences and views and his own, there was such discrepancy. Surely if he had so regarded it, he would not have remained so inactive. As Dr. Jarvis remarks in the document before referred to: "This able and enterprising prelate was never known to pursue a favorite object with an unsteady gaze or an erring aim."

The General Convention of May, 1820, passed a resolution to remove the Seminary to New-Haven. On the fourteenth of July, Bishop Brownell, President *pro tem.*, published, by

order of the Board of Trustees, a plan, preceded by an address, and followed by resolutions.
The address gives a very brief statement of
the original establishment of the Institution.
It then goes on to remark that: "Either from
some defect in the plan, or from objections to
the location, or from some other causes, the
Seminary languished in New-York, and it was
determined by the General Convention to remove it to New-Haven, and to reörganize it
on a different plan." From the plan which follows the address, I transcribe the second and
third sections of the fourth article, which, for
a considerable time, had the force of law, and,
as I well know, were carried into operation.
Subsequently they were rescinded : "Section
II. The Seminary shall be equally accessible to
students of all religious denominations, exhib-
iting suitable testimonials of character and
qualifications. But no one, while a member of
the Institution, shall be permitted to promul-
gate opinions tending to disturb the harmony
of the Protestant Episcopal Church. Section
III. Every student, during his first term of
study, shall be considered as a probationer.
And if, at the end of that time, the professors
shall think him so far deficient in industry, so-
briety, or discretion, as to be unfit to proceed

in his studies, they shall privately direct him to withdraw himself from the institution."

The Seminary was to be reöpened in New-Haven on the thirteenth of September. I had been spending the summer at my father's in Philadelphia, where I had devoted some time to the preparation of an introductory discourse. A few days before the appointed time I went to Jersey City, then called Paulus' Hook. As the yellow fever had made its appearance in some parts of Philadelphia, intercourse with New-York had been interdicted. I therefore hired a boat and was rowed from New-Jersey to the opposite shore north of the city. I landed near what was then the State Prison. Many years after the building was purchased by Mr. Jacob Lorillard, who endeavored to make it a hospital for sick strangers who might desire a suitable boarding-place. He went to great expense in arranging the building so as to accommodate the inmates with every convenience, and in beautifying the grounds. But the enterprise failed. The house still stands in what is now called West-Tenth street, near Washington, and is at present known as the Empire Brewery. At the time I speak of, it was a considerable distance out of town. I found Mr. Warner's carriage waiting for me on the bank, and was conveyed to the country-seat of Mr. John Slidell, a gentleman with whom I had become acquainted during my residence in the city. This was a very pleasant retreat, with a beautiful lawn extending some distance in front to the Bloomingdale road. Now all the ground in that vicinity and far above is thickly built upon. The mansion still stands, and is a large frame building, situated on the north-west corner of the Sixth avenue and Thirtieth street. Here I spent Saturday, and after going on Sunday to a church in the country, passed the night at Camperdown, on the East River, the summer residence of Mr. Isaac Lawrence. In company with this friend of myself and the Seminary, on Monday morning I got on board a steamer bound for New-Haven, where I found the Rev. Jonathan M. Wainwright, John Pintard, Esq., and several other gentlemen who had showed great interest in the Seminary. About sundown we arrived at New-Haven, and the next day I delivered in Trinity Church the introductory discourse, which was published at the request of the Trustees.

After a brief allusion to my feelings on the occasion, I proceeded to show the necessity of an able and well-instructed ministry to the prosperity of the Church. Under the general head of ability were comprehended *piety* and *learning;* and under the latter point, the necessity of a critical and extensive acquaintance with the Scriptures in their original languages was especially insisted on. I then attempted to show that the establishment of theological schools was the most certain method of effecting this desirable object, and referred to the prophetic establishments mentioned in the Old Testament, and to the Jewish and Christian schools of later periods. A brief view of the course of studies intended to be pursued was then presented, the Scriptures and Ecclesiastical History being regarded as comprehending the most important topics. The discourse closed with a short notice of the subject of church government, part of which has already been transcribed.

Thus the General Theological Seminary was commenced in New-Haven on the thirteenth of September, 1820. It opened with ten students, to whom four others were soon added. It appears from the names contained in the report of the Trustees made to the Special General Convention which was called in 1821, that the whole number of students had been twenty-eight. Of those one was "not a regular student, but engaged in teaching a school," another "had leave of absence," three had "left on account of ill-health," and two had been "admitted to orders." Of the original twenty-eight, seventeen are still living, two of whom are Bishops, one a Professor in the Seminary, and others highly respectable rectors of parishes. Of a large majority of the students in New-Haven I can truly say that, during the whole period of my connection with the Institution, I have never known more attentive, studious, thorough, and in every respect decorous young men. Most of them were remarkable for their diligence and application. The public examination which was conducted in Trinity Church in July, 1821, was to me the most satisfactory I ever took part in, and I have reason to think that it made a very favorable impression on all who were present.

The statutes secured to the students a long vacation in the winter. This arrangement was made in order to afford them an opportunity, if desired, of engaging during that time in the business of instruction. I had therefore more than three months at my disposal. Towards the close of the term in 1820, I heard one of the students, now the Rev. Dr. Johnson of

Jamaica, Long Island, read some Hebrew according to the points. This was the first time that I had heard the language so read. On my return to Philadelphia, where I spent the vacation, I set to work to learn the forms of the language, and to read it according to the vowel-points. Unfortunately I had no instructor to keep me right, and therefore lost no little time in making the effort. However, by repeatedly plodding over portions of Robertson's ————*, David Levi's Grammar in his Lingua Sacra, and Bythner's Lyra Prophetica, I managed to get some acquaintance with the Masoretical punctuation, and to read Hebrew slowly according to the old method. On my return to New-Haven in the spring, I endeavored to impart what little knowledge I had to those students who were disposed to take the trouble to learn.

During a considerable portion of the time

---

* NOTE BY THE EDITOR.—One of the following works is doubtless here referred to, but, as we have no means of ascertaining which title ought to fill this blank in the manuscript, we append them all.

Robertson, J. Grammatica Linguæ Hebræ, cum notis. 8vo. Edin. 1758.

Ib. Clavis Pentateuchi. 8vo. Edin. 1770.

Robertson, W. A Key to the Hebrew Bible, by which most of the words are unlocked and opened in an Alphabetical Praxis upon Psalms of David, and Lam. of Jeremiah. 8vo. London 1656.

Ib. Thesaurus Linguæ Sanctæ, seu Concordiantiale Lexicon Hebræo-Latina Biblicum. 4vo. London. 1680.

spent in New-Haven, I met the students every Saturday night in the lecture-room, for critical and devotional purposes alternately. On the latter occasions I either lectured or preached to them; and on the former, one of them read a critical essay, which was the subject of remark by any who might choose to speak in relation to its matter or manner, and also by the professor. One of the critical essays was in Latin, but I am not aware that it elicited any especial comment. We lived together in great harmony, and my feelings were like those of an elder brother helping the younger members of the family. Bishop Brownell attended to the delivery of sermons, and to the department of Pastoral Theology, and met the class once a week. During my continuance in his Diocese he was uniformly kind, hospitable, and friendly; and the residence of his family in New-Haven contributed very much to my satisfaction and enjoyment. In the summer season I frequently visited some neighboring vacant parish and officiated; but generally I attended Trinity Church, of which Dr. Harry Croswell was rector. In the winter the building was excessively cold, as the practice of warming places of worship had not then been introduced in Connecticut.

The Seminary in New-Haven was patronized by many of the leading Churchmen, especially in South-Carolina and New-York City. From those of the latter place particularly, it received extensive presents in books; and the name of John Pintard must ever be most prominent, for the liberality of his donations, and the great number, value, and rarity of the works which adorn its library. Among them I may mention, as specimens, the Bibles of Kennicott, Houbigant, Montanus, and Castalio; the Vulgate of Sixtus V.; and the Paris and Complutensian Polyglots. The last of these is a beautiful and well-preserved copy, in six volumes, which he saw announced in a London catalogue, and for which he paid three hundred dollars. The General Theological Seminary never had a truer friend than this really Christian Churchman, whose religious character was habitually kept warm and active by his expansive benevolence.

Towards the close of July, my sister Eliza, who had lived with me in Maryland, came to New-Haven, to make me a visit, at the house of Mrs. Blagg, with whom I had been boarding, and who was an excellent old lady, the widow of a New-York merchant. On Saturday, the day after the examination, we were about to go to Hartford. I had ordered a conveyance immediately after an early dinner. While it was waiting at the door, the Southern mail came in, and I immediately went to the post-office, a few yards off, to inquire for letters. I received one, informing me of the illness of my father. This of course put a stop to our excursion. About six in the evening, we left New-Haven in the stage, and, after riding all night, arrived at New-York about eight in the morning. There we learned that my sister and Mr. Warner had gone to Philadelphia, and that my father was not expected to recover. We took the mail-stage about two, and, after spending another night in travelling, reached home on Monday morning. Our father had died two days before, on the twenty-sixth day of July, 1821. His illness was short but severe. He spoke to my sister Esther of the time when his pain, which was caused by an inflammation of the bowels, was most severe, as his trying examination-day; showing that his thoughts were turned to what at the same time was engaging my attention, and also that he regarded the chastisement as sent by the Lord, as a trial of his faith. He was indeed a sincere Christian man, full of faith and good works. His views of religion were deep and experimental, and, in the right sense of the word, decidedly evangelical.

My father entered the ministry when about fifty years of age. He had not the advantage of a collegiate education, and therefore all classical examination was dispensed with. He was recommended for holy orders by the Pennsylvania Convention of June twenty-first, 1791, and in the Journal of that held in June fifth, 1792, his name appears as rector of St. Martin's, Marcus Hook. He was ordained by Bishop White, although no report of it by the Diocesan appears in either of the Journals. For his ecclesiastical head he always entertained the most profound respect, and his regard was kindly reciprocated. He and the Rev. Jehu Clay were, for many years, assistant ministers to the Rev. Nicholas Collin, D.D., a Swedish Missionary, who was rector of a church called Wicaco, or Weccacoe,* (now Gloria Dei,) in Southwark, Philadelphia; of another named

---

* I am informed by the Rev. Dr. Clay, the present rector, son of the gentleman above mentioned, that "this was the name at that time, of that particular locality." He supposes both it and "Passyunk, on the Schuylkill, to have been of Indian origin." He remarks also as follows: "At the time this church was built, Dr. Rudman, the first rector, says there was a dispute among the Swedes with regard to the place where it should be erected, those living on the Schuylkill wishing it to be at Passyunk, and those in the vicinity at Wicaco. This seems to show that this locality was called by the latter name." Dr.

Kingsessing, about six miles from the city, near the village of Derby; and a third in Upper Meriom Township, on the Schuylkill, about two miles from Norristown. Dr. Collin had a strong attachment to the Episcopal Church, and a high respect for Bishop White. He and the Episcopal clergy of Philadelphia were on terms of intimate friendship. Indeed, at the time I speak of, any thing like party feeling was unknown. The few city ministers were fraternal in their feelings towards each other, and filial in those towards their ecclesiastical father. However they may have differed on some theoretical points and practical usages, I can truly say that afterwards, during the time of my acquaintance with them, I never heard a harsh word uttered by any one against any other. Every summer, about cherry-time, they all met to spend a friendly evening at my father's, and another at Dr. Collin's. On one of these latter occasions I was present, being a student of divinity, and the Rev. Mr. Barnwell Campbell, who had just arrived from England, read to the clergy Dr. Buchanan's celebrated sermon entitled, *The Star in the*

Clay adds that "the name Gloria Dei, by which the church is now known, occurs occasionally in the early records, and that this is its proper ecclesiastical title."

East. He had been introduced by the Rev. Dr. Abercrombie, who had before become deeply interested in the discourse. It was afterwards printed in Philadelphia, and its circulation produced a favorable impression in behalf of the cause of foreign missions. Mr. Campbell was then quite a young man, of very agreeable and unassuming manners, and of strong religious feeling. His son, who is now a respectable clergyman of Charleston, S. C., has much of his father's character.

Since the death of Dr. Collin, the three churches of which he was rector have become connected with the Episcopal Church. My father, an assistant of Dr. Collin, was also rector of the church at Marcus Hook, a village on the Delaware River, about twenty miles south of Philadelphia, where he officiated once a month. When a boy I was in the habit of accompanying him to the country churches. I also went with him occasionally to Concord, Wilmington, and other places where he happened to officiate. He died in his seventy-ninth year. I may venture to say that few men were more generally and deservedly esteemed.* The crowd that attended his funeral

* I refer you to an obituary notice, (the author of which, I regret to say, is not certainly known to me,) in the *Gospel Advocate*, March, 1822, p. 104.

at St. Paul's Church was so great that it became necessary to keep the gate clear, in order that the procession might have room to enter.

In his will, my father appointed his only surviving son and his two unmarried daughters executor and executrices. Its provisions were carried out with that feeling which ought to characterize near family relationship. On making such arrangements as were advisable from the situation of the property left by him, it became necessary to open three streets, near Catherine, between Second and Fifth. The names by which they were designated, Harmony, Union, and Concord, and which they still bear, were purposely chosen, to indicate the feeling referred to.

CHAPTER VI.

A Diocesan Theological School established in New-York, at the Instance of Bishop Hobart—Jacob Sherred's Legacy—A Special General Convention called to consider it — The Seminary restored to New-York—United with the Diocesan School under a New Organization—Reörganization of the Seminary — First Critical Publication—South-Carolina Trustees suggest a Seminary-Building—Bishop White's Remarks on laying the Corner-Stone—Professor Turner's Marriage — Progress and Character of the Seminary Buildings—Study of the French and German Languages—Revision of our Church Psalmody and Hymns—Translation of "Jahn's Introduction," with Notes — Birth of his First Child — Establishment of Public Worship at the Seminary—Formation of a Sunday-School—St. Peter's Church grows out of these Labors—Studies in Ancient and Modern Languages, and in Rabbinical Writings—Dr. Nordheimer.

WHILE the school of the prophets was pursuing its quiet and retired course, in New-Haven, discussions were going on, and conflicting publications issued elsewhere, respecting the comparative expediency and usefulness of various diocesan institutions or of a general one. The New-York Convention of 1820 had, at the instance of the Bishop, established a "Protestant Episcopal Theological Education Society of the State." This Institution had gone into operation before the meeting of the Convention of

1821, as appears from the Diocesan Address to the Clergy and Laity on that occasion. Its "principal school was placed in the city of New-York, and a branch of it in the village of Geneva," each under its respective professors.

In March, 1821, Mr. Jacob Sherred, a vestryman of Trinity Church, New-York, died, and left a legacy of about sixty thousand dollars to a General Theological Seminary in New-York, or to a diocesan one within the same limits. A suggestion was made, whether the establishment of a General Institution in that diocese would not secure a legal claim to the legacy. The opinion of some of the most distinguished lawyers was decidedly in favor of assigning it to the Education Society. With a view to settle the difficulty a Special General Convention was called, and it was agreed by the respective parties that the General Seminary should be removed to New-York, and a new Institution organized by uniting it with the local school of that diocese. Thus the merging of the two into one was the formation of the present General Theological Seminary.

Bishop Hobart, in whose diocese the Institution was now reörganized and reëstablished, very kindly inquired what position therein would be most acceptable to me. In accordance with what I then stated to him in reply, I was soon after appointed Professor of Biblical Learning and Interpretation of Scripture. For this office, which I have already held more than forty years, I very gratefully express my obligation to the Right Rev. Diocesan, by whose agency I have been enabled, however imperfectly, to assist very many of our clergy in studying the oracles of God, and thus preparing them for the exercise of the ministry, by "bringing out of their treasures things new and old."

In December, 1821, the Trustees published "the Constitution" of the newly organized Seminary, with an "Address to the Protestant Episcopalians of the United States," and "Resolutions," along with a statement of the Professorships "in the city of New-York," and "in the Branch School at Geneva," and some other matters. Bishop Bowen also, of South-Carolina, appealed in behalf of the Seminary, to the Convention of that diocese, held in 1822. A Committee on the subject reported in its favor; and, by desire of the Convention, the Bishop, in an address to the members of his Church, earnestly requested their coöperation. The subject was renewed in 1823, when the same interest was manifested by the Convention of that diocese.

The Faculty of the newly-established Seminary in New-York consisted of the Rev. Bird Wilson, D.D., who had a short time before been appointed by the Trustees to the Department of Systematic Divinity, and myself, of the original General Institution; and also, of the Diocesan School, Bishop Hobart, the Rev. Benjamin T. Onderdonk, Messrs. Clement C. Moore and Gulian C. Verplanck. The branch at Geneva was continued but a short time. The arrangements of the Professorships of this school were very strange. Dr. McDonald was appointed "Professor of *the Interpretation of Scripture*, Ecclesiastical History, and the Nature, Ministry, and Polity of the Church," and "the Rev. John Reed, Professor of *Biblical Learning*." An extraordinary disruption, truly, of one department! From this time the salaries of Dr. Wilson and myself were fifteen hundred dollars each, and of Mr. Moore, seven hundred and fifty dollars. The services of the other gentlemen were gratuitous. Mr. Verplanck, to whom the Evidences of Revealed Religion had been assigned, after some time published his lectures and resigned. Bishop Hobart heard the students read the service and deliver sermons once a week, when his Episcopal duties did not interfere with the arrangement. Mr. Onderdonk, being a regular assistant minister of Trinity Church, found by experience that he could not devote the time which was necessary for suitable preparation in his department, which related to the Church and to Ecclesiastical History. An arrangement was therefore made to relieve him, and Dr. Wilson and myself consented to give, temporarily, instructions in the latter department. This arrangement, which lasted a few years, was originally suggested by Bishop Hobart, and made in accordance with a resolution passed by the Trustees, in reply to a note addressed to that body, July twenty-third, 1822, by Mr. Onderdonk, in which he tendered his "resignation of the department."

I "consented to undertake, for a time, so much of ecclesiastical history as comprises the Old Testament, and the connection between it and the New, together with the first three centuries of the Christian Church." Dr. Wilson took the subsequent period, that of the Reformation being most particularly attended to.*

---

* See our statements in the General Report made by the Faculty to the Trustees, May fourteenth, 1823.

The introductory address on occasion of opening the Seminary in the city of New-York, was delivered in Trinity Church on the evening of March eleventh, 1822, by Bishop Hobart; on the evening of December twenty-seventh, 1822, I delivered an address in the same church; November thirteenth, 1823, Dr. Wilson; and subsequently, Professors Onderdonk and Moore performed the same duty. The classes attended the several professors in rooms of the Trinity Church school, at the corner of Canal and Varick streets, and this arrangement was continued about five years.

Early in May, 1822, having rented a house on the south side of Franklin street next to the corner of Church, I went with my two sisters to live there. We continued there three years, and then removed to Broadway, one door south of Bleecker street, on the east side, where we lived two years.

In 1824 I published in a pamphlet of one hundred and thirty pages, *Notes on the Epistles to the Romans.* I dedicated this, the first of my publications to Bishop White, to whose friendship I always felt that I was indebted for my connection with the Seminary. About thirty or forty copies were sold; the remainder of an issue of seven hundred and fifty I gave away, chiefly to students of the Seminary, whom I supplied for several years. In this work, (for I may so call it, as no little labor was bestowed upon it,) I committed the practical error of too much brevity, from a desire of producing the matter in a cheap form. If this did not occasion obscurity, it resulted in a production which required more trouble to examine than even clergymen and candidates were disposed to give. As my old friend, Dr. Henry Lyon Davis, told me, it demanded too much from the reader. The Greek words were printed in a very contracted form, only two or three of the first letters being given. Numerous texts, necessary to be examined in order to perceive their bearing on the interpretation which they were intended to confirm, were merely referred to. The book was rather favorably noticed in an English periodical. But the reviewer charged the author with a good many erroneous interpretations. Had he taken the trouble to read through the notes which contained them, he would have found that in almost all the cases specified, these interpretations were stated as having been given by some previous commentators, and that the author had attempted to set them aside, and to establish what he regarded as the true meaning. The reviewer, like very many of his brethren, had lightly skimmed over the book without diving below its surface.

At a meeting of the trustees held on July twenty-seventh, 1824, "a communication from the South-Carolina trustees," signed by Bishop Bowen and six other gentlemen, was read, recommending "that measures be adopted for providing the Seminary as soon as possible, with its own proper habitation," and proposing to erect a suitable edifice on the ground given by Professor Moore. On the following day it was resolved to erect such a building, and a committee of five was "appointed to report the proper measures for carrying the resolution into effect." On the twenty-eighth of July, 1825, "the trustees assembled at the residence of Professor Moore, and with the faculty, students, clergy, and an assemblage of citizens, formed a procession to the site of the intended building, where after an address and prayers by the Presiding Bishop, the corner-stone was laid by him, assisted by Bishop Kemp, Bishop Croes, and Bishop Brownell." In the address Bishop White expresses his joy on the occasion. At the same time he declares that "he would deprecate the laying of one stone upon another, and would withdraw his hand from the laying of the first stone, if he could foresee that in the instruction to be given in the building, there would at any future time — at present there is no danger of it — be a departure from those properties of system, in doctrine, in discipline, and in worship, which in the sixteenth century were cleared from superstition by the leaders in the English Reformation, were brought to the colonies, recognized by us in the organization of our American Church, and under the influence of the grace of God, have been persevered in by us to the present day." This allusion to the errors of Popery, and avowal of the fundamental principles of Protestantism, as recognized by the reformed Church of England, are entirely in harmony with the sentiments and feeling which were habitually cherished by this most distinguished Bishop of our Church. He then proceeds to " request every person present to put up a mental prayer to the Bestower of all good, so to govern the minds of those who now or who may hereafter superintend the studies of the Institution, as that they may furnish the gold, the silver, and the precious stones of sound doctrine, to the exclusion of the wood, the hay, and the stubble of human imperfection, and that the labors to be bestowed may endure the fire of that great day which shall try every man's work of what sort it is." The service of the occasion was concluded with the Lord's Prayer, some appropriate collects, and a prayer for the Seminary.

In the year 1825 I formed an acquaintance with Mary Esther, second daughter of Burrage Beach, Esq., of Cheshire, Connecticut. The loveliness both of person and character, which made this dear one a favorite with all who knew her, soon produced in me its natural result, and I became deeply attached to her. To my great joy she reciprocated the feeling, and on the twenty-third of May, 1826, we were married in Cheshire by the Rev. Tillotson Bronson, D.D., an old friend of the family. My domestic happiness was now completed, and I seemed to myself to have become a new and settled man. I felt now that my motives to industry were increased, and that I never could do enough to show my gratitude to divine Providence, and my love to one who had consented to become my companion and comforter through life.

The erection of the Seminary building, the corner-stone of which had been laid in 1825, was delayed for a considerable time, so that it was not in a condition to be occupied until

C

late in the spring of 1827. It is the present east building, about one hundred feet long and fifty deep. Each end is a convenient house for a professor, the west being that which I selected for a dwelling, and the middle part so arranged as to provide rooms in the basement for the janitor's family, and a large apartment on the left of the hall for a library. The remaining portion is divided into rooms for the students. The edifice is rather unsightly. A rude attempt was made to give it something of a Gothic appearance by supplying it with eight rough buttresses, and attaching wooden fixtures like mullions outside of very plain window-sashes with square angles. The shingled roof was surrounded by a wooden parapet, and the eight buttresses terminated by wooden conical turrets. These and other similar appendages have since been removed. Bishop Hobart, who had not been on the ground, from the time that the corner-stone was laid, until I had become established in the house appropriated to me, having been, during part of the time, in Europe, expressed in my hearing his feelings of disappointment in brief but most marked language. Those who are acquainted with the present site and appearance of the Seminary, will be surprised to learn that the building lay in a hollow. The carriage-entrance thereto, which was in what is now the Ninth Avenue, about half-way between Twentieth and Twenty-first streets, was about fifteen feet higher than the spot on which the edifice stood, and in some places the ground was eighteen feet above it. We drove down the short hill through a small apple-orchard, and riding behind the building came round in front of the west entrance. There was then no street in the neighborhood. We were in the country, and the village of Greenwich lay between us and the city. One southern road led into it, which is the present Ninth Avenue and Hudson street, and another called Love Lane, (now Twenty-first street,) ran an easterly course to the Bloomingdale road. The Hudson River at high tide washed what is now the Tenth Avenue, and even a portion of the lot east of it. During the winter the water was sometimes ankle deep in front of the house, so that in order to have a dry access to the lecture-room, in the centre of the building, I had a door cut through the garret partition. One winter the mud was so deep immediately around the building as to make it almost inaccessible, except on horseback or in a carriage. At the time that I removed into the Seminary building there was hardly a good three-story brick house all the way to Canal street. In course of time the grounds were reduced to the present level, which is considerably above that of the adjoining streets; the low lots on the river, and even a considerable distance into it, were filled in, and the whole block beautifully ornamented with trees and shrubbery. For the last-mentioned improvement we were indebted to Mr. James MacFarlan, a leading and active member of the Board.

I must now go back to mention some other matters of a private nature. It was not until the year 1819 or 1820, after I had entered upon the duties of my professorship in the Seminary, that I began to learn the French language under a native instructor in New-York. Four or five years after, I commenced the study of German, along with the Rev. Manton Eastburn, who at that time was assistant minister to Dr. Lyell, in Christ Church. Our teacher was a highly-respected Lutheran clergyman, of German extraction, though a native of Philadelphia, and a good scholar, well known and esteemed in the community. But he lacked one all-important qualification of a teacher, namely, ability to communicate knowledge with clearness and definiteness.

We left him, therefore, at the expiration of one quarter, and I pursued the study for a time alone, and afterwards with the assistance of a native, who, however, showed the same incompetency. The importance of this language to readers in general, and particularly to a biblical student, induced me to devote much time to it. I only regret that my attention had not been directed to this and other modern languages earlier in life.

Having been appointed, by the General Convention, a member of a committee to prepare and submit for their action a suitable collection of Hymns to be used in public worship, and also to make selections for the same purpose from Tate and Brady's version of the Psalms, with such alterations as might be thought necessary or expedient—in 1825 or '26 —I employed some of my leisure time in attending to this duty. With the version before mentioned I compared carefully our Bible and Common Prayer Book translations; also Dathe's Latin Translation, and the Septuagint and Hebrew. I think, also, that I made use of Luther's German. The result of these comparisons I embodied in certain communications which were published in one of our Church periodicals of the day. I was thus enabled to suggest alterations in the language, and occasionally in the sentiment of that portion of the old metrical Psalter which is still in use; and as several of them were adopted by the Committee, and incorporated into the version, I presume that they may be regarded as improvements.

An alumnus of the Seminary, William R. Whittingham, who, while a pupil, had distinguished himself for careful preparation, thorough research, and conscientious discharge of every duty, and who, since his admission into the ministry, has further distinguished himself as a prominent man, in the highest ecclesiastical body of the Church, assented to a proposal of coöperating with me in preparing for the press a translation of Jahn's Introduction to the Old Testament. The author's Latin work was made the basis, but the larger German was also carefully examined, and a considerable proportion of its more important matter was incorporated partly in the text, but chiefly in notes. The translators, also appended notes of their own, and in those cases particularly, where they thought it important to correct certain loose or doubtful views of the author. Once, at the urgent request of Mr. Whittingham, I consented to add the initial of my name to a note of some length, which I had prepared on the Samaritan Pentateuch. Both translation and notes, however, were throughout examined by both of us, and in the Preface we acknowledged ourselves "responsible for every part." The book was published by the Carvills, in an octavo volume of five hundred and forty-six pages. So little interest has been taken in the critical study of the Old Testament that a second edition has never been published. Yet it embodies more biblical information relating to the Old Testament than any other book of its size.

On the seventeenth of October, 1827, about six months after our establishment in the Seminary building, our first child was born. She was baptized by the Right Rev. Bishop Hobart, D.D., on Sunday afternoon, December thirtieth, 1827, in the Chapel of the Theological Seminary, and named after her maternal grandmother, Julia Beach. The prayer, which, on recording her birth in the folio edition of the Bible, Edinburgh, 1793, which came to me with other books of my father's, I also recorded, namely, "that we may educate her as a good Christian and acccomplished woman, and that God may spare her to be a comfort to our future years," the wise Controller of all things thought it best not to grant. This our first child was taken to her heavenly Father on the second of April, a quarter after two A.M., 1831. She died of scarlet fever, after a short illness of thirty-five hours, on the morning after Good Friday, having been apparently quite well the day before. She was an interesting and lovely child, of more than ordinary intelligence for her years, and very sweet and amiable in her disposition. Her remarkable precocity of mind, the tenacity of her memory, which enabled her to retain many hymns and little poetic pieces taught her by her mother and aunts, and her admiration of the beauties of nature, which she would often express when observing a glorious sunset, made her attractive to and beloved by all our friends. The last articulate sounds that she uttered were those of the Lord's Prayer. Her death was a heavy blow to us, but I may truly say that we both acquiesced in the will of God, assured that His providential dispensation must be right, however inadequately we could see its true scope and purpose.

The long room, in the middle part of the Seminary, which was appropriated for a Library, and which is still used for the same purpose, was the professors' only lecture and recitation-room. There we generally attended the classes, accommodating each other as to time. Subsequently, however, we found it necessary to make use of one of the basement rooms, which had been occupied by the janitor, and is so still. As the walls of the Library afforded more than ample space for the books, and consequently the whole middle part was free, Dr. Wilson and myself, the same year that I removed to the Seminary, established there a regular Sunday-morning service. It was attended by our families, also by that of Professor Moore, who resided in the immediate neighborhood, by the students, and some of the residents of the vicinity. A Sunday-school was soon formed, in which several of the students took an active part. Some ladies also showed a lively interest in this good work; among whom may be mentioned Dr. Moore's two elder daughters, Miss Martin, who superintended Dr. Wilson's domestic establishment, and my sister Eliza. The school became very flourishing, and the little congregation increased, so that in a few years a parish was organized. St. Peter's Chapel was built, and the Rev. Benjamin I. Haight, who had just finished his course in the Seminary, took charge of the congregation in 1831 or '32. He was succeeded by an English clergyman, the Rev. Mr. Pyne, and he by Dr. Hugh Smith, in the commencement of whose rectorship St. Peter's Church was built, the chapel being altered into a house for the rector. Thus the few people who assembled for worship in the Library, and the Sunday scholars who were there taught, were the nucleus of the congregation of that church.

During my previous residence in the city and afterwards at the Seminary I devoted my leisure time principally to study, reviewed a good many Latin classics, read Homer's Iliad through, kept up a regular course of German reading, especially in Schiller, with a large portion of whose works I became quite familiar, studied the Old Testament in Hebrew, with the Chaldee portions, also attended to the Syriac language, and read in it the Gospel of St. John, and some other parts of the New Testament. During the same time I devoted much attention to Rabbinic. I made unassisted efforts to read and understand the Commentaries of Jarchi and D. Kimchi, but found them, especially the former, wholly dark and unintelligible. After some time I procured the aid of a well-instructed Polish Jew, Posnanski, and again of a German named Barschall, a good

Rabbinical scholar, who endeavored to make me pay fifty dollars for ten hours' instruction, but was obliged to content himself with half the amount. After a while I became acquainted with Dr. Nordheimer, the author of a valuable Hebrew Grammar, who unhappily was cut off in the midst of a career of literary biblical usefulness. He was a deeply-read Jew, an honorable man, who made no pretense of a conversion to Christianity, although he was by no means an advocate of Talmudical fables and extravagance. We read together some time, and I also began with him the study of Arabic. In course of time, I read by myself Locman's Fables, and two Suras of the Koran, making use of Kosegarten's Glossary, and Giggeio's Lexicon in four folio volumes. This last work I imported from England, having seen it announced for sale in a London catalogue. It is dedicated to the Holy Ghost, the author of the gift of tongues! I had a fine copy of Marracci's Koran, which has become exceedingly scarce. I regret very much that, after some years, the pressure of various duties, together with other circumstances, led me to neglect the study of these languages. I believe that the practice of reading a Rabbinical commentary, in rather small print, at night, weakened my eyes. A painful attack, occasioned by a cold, lasting about ten days, compelled me to use them with great caution and moderation, and soon after I was obliged to resort to spectacles. In general, however, I have been greatly blessed with good sight; for which 1 desire to be duly thankful.

CHAPTER VII.

Clerical Association in New-York—Object of it—Constitution —Bishop Hobart's Attack upon it—Dr. Turner's Reply— The Course pursued by the Members — Erroneous Impressions—Essays, etc., in Biblical Literature.

In the spring of the year 1829, an unpleasant affair occurred, which I think proper to relate somewhat in detail, inasmuch as its history and development involve some principles of importance.

A few of my clerical brethren, feeling desirous of contributing to their mutual improvement, both in religious character and theological knowledge, agreed to meet each other at stated times to converse on some topic of divinity, or religion, or pastoral duty, previously proposed and adopted for consideration. The members were to assemble in turn at each other's houses, take tea together, and after uniting in prayer — appropriate selections having been made from an English publication—communicate their respective views and thoughts upon the particular point which had been previously agreed on. In order to carry out their object the more effectually, they adopted the following very simple Constitution, and had a moderate number of copies printed, together with the forms of prayer, for the use of the members:

CONSTITUTION.

"*Article* 1. This Association shall be called *The Protestant Episcopal Clerical Association of the City of New-York*, and shall have for its object the promotion of the personal piety and the official usefulness of its members, by devotional exercises, and by conversation on missionary and such other religious subjects, as may conduce to mutual edification.

"*Article* 2. There shall be attached to this Association a Secretary, who shall be one of the members. He may be elected annually, and shall continue in office until a successor be chosen. It shall be his duty to keep a record of the members of the Association, the times and places of its meetings, the subjects considered, and such other things as may from time to time be directed. He shall call special meetings of the Association at the request of any three of its members.

"*Article* 3. None but clergymen of the Protestant Episcopal Church may be members of this Association. Any such clergyman in the city of New-York, or its vicinity, may become a member by signifying his disposition in writing to the Secretary, with his approbation of the nature and object of the Association. Any member has liberty to invite a Protestant Episcopal minister, not resident in the city of New-York or its vicinity, to attend any of the regular meetings of the Association.

"*Article* 4. Every meeting of the Association shall be opened and concluded with a form of prayer; and the member at whose house the meeting is held shall preside.

"*Article* 5. This Constitution may be altered only by a vote of two thirds of the members of the Association."

The whole number of clergymen thus associating was ten, alphabetically as follows: the Rev. Drs. or Messrs. Cruse, Eastburn, Evan Johnson, McIlvaine, Milnor, Muhlenberg, Schroeder, Seabury, Turner, and Wainwright. As the Association continued in existence a very short period, it received no accessions.

The prospect of meeting such a friendly and fraternal company, for a purpose so good and laudable, was very gratifying to me. I had long thought that the clergy of the Episcopal Church did not sufficiently confer together in reference to the practical duties of their profession, and to their own advancement in theological knowledge. I had no doubt that more frequent and familiar intercourse, and a free and friendly interchange of sentiment, would tend to bring out the numerous important points in which they agreed, and, by a clear exposition of the varied phraseology in use, would show also that the real differences of opinion were neither numerous nor weighty. The few occasions on which I was present with the Association were very agreeable, and, as it appeared to me, gave decided evidence of a useful tendency, both in imparting information and in eliciting thought and knowledge.

The Society had been in operation only a few weeks, when, to my utter surprise and amazement, the Bishop of the diocese issued a pastoral letter addressed to its clergy and laity, objecting to the Association, and warning against it. In private conversation with Drs. Milnor and Wainwright, the Bishop had " *unofficially*" objected to the formation of such an association. As my residence was then in a very retired position, I had not heard of his expressed opposition, and therefore, when his published letter came to me, I actually looked twice at the title before I could feel satisfied that our Clerical Association was what he intended to denounce. That an Association in itself so harmless, and in its tendencies so beneficial, should have been publicly attacked by the highest ecclesiastical authority of the diocese, and held up as a thing to be shunned, appeared scarcely credible.

After noting the definite name, "*The* Association," as a "title" which "a minority of the clergy have thought themselves warranted in assuming for *their* Association, of which the Bishop and a large majority of the Protestant Episcopal clergy of the city have declined being or are not members," and making some general introductory remarks, the letter proceeds to give the diocesan's reasons for considering the plan of such an association "*inexpedient* and *unnecessary.*"

"1. Though every clergyman should aim at the greatest piety and zeal, and with this view should devote himself, habitually and earnestly and fervently, to private reading, meditation, and prayer, and should avail himself of *occasional* opportunities of counsel and converse with his brethren; yet, organized clerical associations for prayer and spiritual conversation, and expounding of Scripture, have a strong tendency to become the theatres of spiritual vanity and ostentation, and of that peculiar and artificial language of religion,.which is significantly denoted by the term *cant;* and than which, there is not any thing more offensive to the delicacy, simplicity, and purity of genuine piety.

2. "In these associations, *excitement* is the object." This being presumed, the inference is thus stated: "The heats of enthusiasm will soon influence religious conversation; reason may remonstrate—but what is the still, small voice of reason amidst the storms of enthusiasm?" Appeal is made to "the history of the Church of England in the reigns of Elizabeth and the first Charles," with a special reference to the celebrated *"prophesyings,"* and also to the rise of Methodism.

3. The Bishop expresses his approbation of *"conversation* on religious subjects, in the ordinary course of those occasional meetings which clergymen always have;" but objects to it at "a meeting organized with its presiding officer, its secretary, its book of minutes, etc., etc., in which I *must* talk spiritually, in which I am to *prepare* to talk spiritually, in which the emulation may be, who can talk *most* spiritually. Well will it be, if *discussion* begun for 'mutual edification,' does not end in mutual strife."

4. He objects chiefly to such associations, because "they may be made the powerful *instruments of intrigue, and engines of party.*" He does not assert, however, that " such is the tendency or design of the particular" one in question, or even the "*capability* of any individual connected with it." Only supposing an impetus to be given, and "the power that gives it to be acquired by one or more members of these associations, and who will say that they will not be made the instruments of faction ? Most are they to be dreaded under the *popular form* in which, in many respects, our Church is in this country organized. Our bishops are elective; various officers intrusted with important duties, standing committees, etc., etc., are elective. It is of great importance to guard against the operations of faction and party influence."

5. Another objection is thus expressed: "These associations for promoting personal piety and mutual edification, by devotional exercises and religious conversation, etc., will become not only the instruments, but the invidious *badges* of *party*. Those who engage in them, however they may disclaim the representation, will be held up as more evangelical, more spiritual, more devoted to their Master's service, than those who do not avail themselves

of these plausible means of personal piety and mutual edification." The Bishop argues against such an association, because it may produce evils of the kind stated. He had expected that the intention of forming the Association would be abandoned in consequence of his private representation made to the two clergymen before mentioned. "On the ministers of Christ this ready relinquishment of whatever is *not essential*, in deference to the wishes, the feelings, and the characters of a respectable portion of their brethren, and of him who is set over them in the Lord, seemed to him an imperative act of delicacy, kindness, and duty, not permitting a moment's hesitation."

The above is a condensed but faithful statement of all the reasoning contained in the pastoral letter, and expressed, for the most part, in its own words.

On the appearance of the pastoral letter, the Association thought it right to publish the Constitution and prayers, which before had been "printed exclusively for their own use, and, with the exception of half-a-dozen copies at most, retained in their own possession." To them were now prefixed a few "Prefatory Remarks." These remarks gave occasion to a pamphlet issued under the title: "A Vindication of the Pastoral Letter from the Animadversions contained in the 'Prefatory Remarks,'" etc. Some mistakes in point of fact and doctrine in the Vindication, were corrected in an addition appended to "the Account," a notice of which will immediately be given.

In consequence of this *publicly* announced opposition of the Bishop, Dr. Wainwright, who had been on terms of close intimacy with him, and who was the rector of Grace Church, thought it a duty to relinquish his connection with the Society. Mr. Schroeder also, being associated with the Bishop as an assistant minister of Trinity Parish, felt himself to be in a very delicate position. It was apprehended too, and not without reason, that if the Association were continued, notwithstanding the avowed opposition of the Bishop and such of the clergy as harmonized with him on the subject, it could hardly fail to become the organ of a party. For now no clergymen would attach themselves to it, who were not ready or willing to come in collision with the Bishop, and therefore any accession which it might hereafter gain, would be altogether of Churchmen of one particular stamp. The members were unwilling to subject the Association to such a dilemma, and therefore they came to the conclusion that, simply on the ground of expediency, it would be best to dissolve it. The nature of this reason, as it involved a point of extreme delicacy, they could not fully develop and publish freely to the world. This would have been to proclaim their reluctance that the Association should be composed almost exclusively of one of the two leading classes. Yet I know that this consideration had no slight weight in determining their judgment as to the expediency of dissolving.

But they could not think of dissolving without vindicating what they had done. It was therefore determined to issue a publication to this effect, and to defend the Association from the Bishop's objections. The obligation of preparing the reply was imposed on me. I undertook it, as the agent and spokesman of the union, and because I felt it to be a serious duty to give publicity to what I then believed and do now believe to be the simple truth of the case. I spoke my mind respectfully but plainly, claiming what I regarded as every sincere and intelligent Christian man's right, which, also, the Reformation had recognized, and showing the inadequacy of the reasoning in the pastoral letter. When the paper was read to the members, some expressions were thought to be too strong, and therefore objected to by Dr. Milnor, and one or two others. They were consequently modified. Mr. Seabury's opinion was, that the statements were not strong enough. In other respects also he seemed to think that the paper needed alteration. At my request, he took and examined it, but returned it unaltered. Subsequently, in a very friendly letter which he wrote me, and which I shall have occasion hereafter to quote, he thanks me for what I had done, and expresses a "high degree of satisfaction at the manner in which it had been executed." With such modifications as have been alluded to, the paper was accepted, and directed to be published with the following title: "Account of the True Nature and Object of the late Protestant Episcopal Clerical Association of the City of New-York, together with a Defense of the Association from objections which have been urged against it, and an explanation of the reasons which have led to its dissolution. By THE MEMBERS OF THE ASSOCIATION. 'Let every man be fully persuaded in his own mind.' St. Paul." I shall endeavor to give a brief but fair statement of its contents.

The publication begins by requesting of the "reader a candid examination of the subject, with unbiassed reflection on its nature, on the principles it involves, and on the results to which it leads." It states the motives which produced it: "We have no intention or wish to disturb the harmony of the Church. Those who have known us longest and most intimately will, we are confident, do us justice on this point; and against some of us calumny has never dared to make the charge.

"Neither do we wish to wound the feelings or lessen the proper and legitimate influence of the Bishop. Could we effect such an object, its attainment would recoil upon ourselves with tenfold force, and injury inflicted on the head would effectually destroy the members."

After disavowing any desire "to gratify corrupt and malignant passions," the positive motives are stated.

1. "A *sacred* regard to truth;" a wish to correct "impressions with respect to the nature of the Association" which are "entirely unfounded, and views strangely and grossly erroneous."

2. "An *honorable* regard to our own characters and influence; the esteem of wise and good men" being of "intrinsic value, and the respect of the members of (our) Church absolutely essential to our usefulness."

3. "An *affectionate* regard to the pious part of our ecclesiastical community." In connection with this point, a reference is made, bearing on the application of the term *cant*, which is represented as "the legitimate offspring of ignorance and fanaticism, whether it be associated with the most ardent piety, when it is misnamed *religious*, or whether it is leagued on the side of indecision, indulgence, and sin, when it is properly to be denominated the *cant of the world.*"

4. "A *sincere* regard for the best interests of the Protestant Episcopal Church in the United States. Any aberration from her moderate and conciliatory principles, any deviation from her enlarged spirit and noble magnanimity, shown by directly or indirectly discouraging the exercise of rights, which neither her principles or usages have ever withheld from her clergy in general, would be injurious to her influence and extension any where, and especially in such a country as ours."

The account then proceeds to state "the object of the Association," and the desire of several clergymen, among whom was the late rector of St. Thomas's Church, the Rev. Cornelius Duffie, for such meetings. The Bishop's advice was given in *friendship*, and was never regarded in any other light than as a private expression of opinion. The publication of "his pastoral letter without any communication with the Association, either orally or in writing," was "not merely to the surprise but to the utter astonishment of every member, some of whom would not believe the rumor of its publication when it reached them." Then follow the Constitution, and a brief specimen of the minutes of a meeting; introduced to correct known misapprehensions, which had been received, if not misstatements which had been circulated.

"The members" then proceed to "point out to the reader the objects which the Association had in view."

The "first was to promote piety in themselves, in their brethren, and thus indirectly in their congregations." They repel the charge of intimating want of it in their brethren, but maintain that, "however great may be the piety of the clergy, it is for the good of themselves and of the Church at large, to be habitually increasing it."

Their "second object was, to improve in knowledge connected with their profession." The importance of such improvement is illustrated. "Superficial knowledge is sure to produce superficial preaching, because it can not instruct, and consequently can not permanently impress a rational creature."

"Another object" hoped for was, "the promotion of harmony of feeling, of character, and, in a measure, of views of Christian doctrine. The members did not doubt that good men, of different views, by being brought together, might be led to form a more favorable estimate of each other's character, and that thus a spirit of conciliation would be mutually excited, unkind suspicions removed, and charity enkindled in each breast."

Such being "the nature and objects of the Association," they ask whether "it is really necessary to defend it? *With an object acknowledged to be good, with ties of unity confessedly of the strongest kind, with no other prayers than such as are granted to be adapted to the end in view, might it not have been expected that something should have been yielded to the influence of gentlemanly and Christian feelings, coöperating with assistance from above, to restrain any member of such an Association from running into the evils assumed to be its natural result?* We are compelled to regard the subject in a very different light from our diocesan."

Dr. Wainwright's letter is then given in full, containing the reasons of his determination to leave the Association. A few observations on the letter are appended, with the view of doing justice to the writer, and also of presenting certain points in which the members dissented from him. It states also the reasons which led them to dissolve the institution. The disconnection of Dr. Wainwright would tend to prevent accessions to the body. They would be subjected to censure for continuing in opposition to the Bishop's publicly expressed wish, and exposed to the charge of party feeling. The pastoral letter would, no doubt, become the occasion of frustrating the main purposes of the organization. "Such are our reasons for dissolving. Not that we are convinced of the injurious tendency of the Association; not that we admit the obligation of acquiescing in the views of the Bishop, on matters left free to individual judgment by the wisdom of the Church; not that we admit that, in consequence of the dilemma in which the pastoral letter placed us, more evil than good would necessarily have resulted from continuing. We do not thereby consider ourselves as in any measure pledged to form no similar association, so long as the *laws* of the Church leave us in this respect free to exercise our own judgments. *Legislative enactments* we will always obey, provided they are not opposed to the requisitions of our consciences."

The members of the Association felt that a proper sense of self-respect required them to vindicate themselves " from the charges that had been brought against them." They begin by noting "the impression which the pastoral letter of a Bishop, printed and published, will naturally produce on a large body of the community. In the present case it must tend to our disadvantage. We do not speak of its *design;* we speak of its *tendency.* No man can doubt, for a moment, that the expression of disapprobation, through such a channel, is virtually a *public admonition.*"

They then take up the various objections, as before given from the pastoral letter under their respective numbers. Previously, however, they set aside the censure on the title, by remarking, that, if the indefinite article had been used it might have given rise to the inquiry, " Is this only *one of several clerical associations?* or, *is it in contemplation to form other such?*" and also that other societies are designated in the same way, as, for instance, " *The* Literary and Philosophical Society—*The*

Historical Society;" such phraseology being sanctioned by usage.

1. The fact of the Association being organized does not prove it to have the *tendency* with which it is charged. There is no " connection between organization and *cant*." The evils apprehended may exist as well " without a constitution as with one, in '*occasional*' meetings of the clergy as in regular; in conversation on religious topics when a party of clergymen meet incidentally, as when they meet for the purpose. The truth is, the consequence of which the Bishop thus expresses his apprehension, is only to be feared upon the supposition that the clergy should become a set of ignorant enthusiasts." Had there been no constitution, " what pledge would we have given to each other or to the Church, that our ' Association' should be ' Protestant,' or ' Episcopal,' or ' clerical ?' How could we have provided against the admission of non-Episcopal members ?" If " nothing had been determined as to the manner in which the devotions should be conducted, would it not have been objected with reason, that we were not at all solicitous to conform to the usages of our own Church ? that we had taken no pains to guard against

the mischiefs which would flow from indiscriminate extemporaneous prayer?"

2. The second objection is set aside by denying that such extravagant results are "reasonably to be expected from clergymen of the Protestant Episcopal Church meeting at stated times, under the simplest of constitutions, for the harmless purpose of praying together with a form, of conversing together, as men of *tolerably* good sense at least, on subjects connected with their profession." The excitement aimed at is not *animal*, but that "of religious *thought* and *sensibility*." The cases referred to in the history of England are totally different from the present, and therefore irrelevant.

3. This objection is like the first. "As to any obligation to talk spiritually, we remark that all conversation is voluntary, being neither more nor less than the intercourse of friends. As to the inference drawn from '*preparing* to talk spiritually,' it proves too much." Carried to its legitimate extent, it would sanction the objection of Quakers to "our church service." 'Discussion may end in strife.' This "we can not deny. But we must not be expected to see force in arguments founded on possibilities. According to such a method of reasoning, we ask, what institution, divine or human, can

escape censure? If the abuse of a thing is an an argument against its use, every thing is over thrown. Government has been abused, religion has been abused, Christianity itself has been abused." The cause of the evil is then shown. "But we assume in our defense that clergymen are not worse than other men." If "physicians, gentlemen of the bar, votaries of science or literature, associate for purposes" of improvement, "are ministers of the Gospel the only set of men who are not to be restrained by the courtesies of life or the influence of their religion?" If this be at all true, then it is "one of the strongest reasons in favor of discussion," inasmuch as it may become the occasion of bringing them to a better state of mind.

4. "The argument" of this objection, "is founded in the apprehension that the *character of the Association may change*, or that it might be regarded *as a precedent* for the formation of others, with *different objects and tendencies*." This is barely a conceivable case, but destitute of any probability. The same may be conceived of any institution. We must trust somewhat to the integrity of man, and the superintendence of Providence, to control such possible evils. The Bishop's argument presumes an impetus in a wrong direc-

tion. But "why should we take it for granted that the impetus *must* be wrong? We admit all that the language states. Any association will move with force in the direction of
the impetus given it. The argument *takes it
for granted* that the characters of the members, giving the impetus, will be factious." This
is the very thing to be proved. "The security
against faction and all its baleful evils, lies in
elevating the clerical character both in intellectual ability and personal religion."

5. As the reply to the Bishop's remarks under this head is very full and plain, and as it
avows some most important principles which
the members of the Association were prepared
to claim, defend and act upon, I think it best
to transcribe almost the whole answer.

"The reasoning is of this nature. 'Of a
number of professional men, a considerable
proportion or a few, as the case may be, are
of opinion that certain measures are beneficial,
and therefore determine to adopt them. Others who think differently, or who, agreeing in
the beneficial tendency of the measures, are
nevertheless indisposed to pursue them, object
that the conduct of the other members of the
fraternity is in this respect peculiar, that it
leads to invidious distinctions, etc.' Are those

7*

men who urge this argument willing to yield to its legitimate consequences ? Who does not see that it strikes at the root of all improvement ? A professor in a college, must limit his studies to the measure of literature required by his brethren of the faculty, lest he should be suspected of aiming at distinction above his equals, and thus give rise to jealousies and mutual criminations. A clergyman in a parish must preach no oftener than those of his vicinity, must promote no more objects of usefulness than those which they think proper to engage in, lest invidious comparisons should be made, and ' party spirit be engendered.' If one clergyman have more ability, more strength—whether corporeal or mental—than another, he is not to use it in his Master's service, lest he should thereby become distinguished among his fellows, and ' be held up' as possessed of superior endowments. This, we think, is the fair and natural issue of the argument. Let it be applied to the case of the *first* clergyman who attempted to raise in his congregation a society for distributing the Scriptures and Book of Common Prayer, or a Missionary Society, or a Bible-class, or even a Sunday-school. If his brethren of the vicinity differ from him as to any one of these objects, the reasoning might be urged with the same force: 'Those who engage in them will be held up as more evangelical.'

"There is one point advanced under this head to which we respectfully and earnestly solicit the attention of our clerical and lay brethren. The principle is stated as prescribing a correct line of conduct for the clergy to pursue. It is comprehended in the following sentence: ' On the ministers,' etc., p. 68.

"Here is a *rule of action* for the clergy, which, together with the *laws* prescribed by the Church, (which all must consider themselves bound to *obey*,) will never allow them to be at a loss as to the course of their duty. Is there any matter which the *laws of the Church* have left to individual judgment, and does a presbyter wish to know how to conduct himself in relation to it? · He has only to consult ' the wishes and feelings of a respectable portion of his brethren, and of him who is set over them,' together with the effect which the object in view may be supposed by them to have on their ' characters ;' and it becomes an ' *imperative* act of delicacy, kindness, and DUTY, not permitting a moment's hesitation,' to comply with them. How completely by this process is the whole course of ministerial conduct subjected to the will of a few individuals, not to say of him who presides; for no man can doubt where, under the circumstances referred to, the 'deference' is to be shown. It will be said, that the doctrine limits its application to matters '*non-essential.*' But it may be asked, what is to be understood by *essential?* It is a relative term, and what is *essential* in reference to one end is *indifferent* with respect to another. It is an inquiry of more importance—who is to decide whether a matter is essential or not? Not the persons engaged in it, but the Bishop and such as choose to agree with him. Now what is the result of such a system? Plainly this: *that not one step can be taken by any presbyter, in points where the Church has left him free to act according to his own impressions of duty, without a liability to have his measures reversed.* Where no law restrains, the *opinion* of the Bishop, especially if supported by ' a respectable portion' of the clergy, is propounded with an equal claim to deference, upon grounds which come home to a man of feeling just in proportion as his sensibility gets the better of his judgment; and propounded under peril, not of ecclesiastical penalties, for the Church has threatened none, but of being held up to the public as refractory in 'duty,' and 'pertinacious' in zeal. If a few ministers of God may not organize themselves into a society, not for the purpose of a competition of 'prophesyings' (so called) before a public assembly, but for prayer and religious conversation in the unostentatious privacy of their own dwellings, without causing as great pain to the Bishop as any one 'of the harassing events of a trying Episcopate of eighteen years has given him;' and if, upon continuing the measure after the Bishop's expression of his disapprobation, they are to be exposed to a public arraignment before the clergy and laity of the Church, it is difficult to conceive how any course of conduct, be it ever so blameless, may not become the subject of similar animadversion."

The operation of the principle laid down by the Bishop is then subjected to two practical tests, in order to illustrate its bearing and operation. Afterwards the reply proceeds thus:

"Against such a principle, therefore, we respectfully but firmly protest. We will yield great deference to the judgments of those who are or may be 'set over us in the Lord,' whether privately or publicly expressed; but we claim the right, which the Church has not taken from us, of examining the alleged reasons and forming our own opinions."

In confirmation of the view taken by the members of the Association, of the meaning of the word "duty," as intended by the Bishop, a passage is quoted from a pamphlet, which had just been published, entitled: "A Vindication of the Pastoral Letter." Speaking of "*the deference due to the Bishop*," the author makes these remarks: "Some contend, and very faithfully and uniformly practise upon the principle, that even in unessential points no obedience is due to him; and that his 'admonitions' and his 'judgment' are in no case, when differing from theirs, to be heeded. Is this left free by the Church to individual judgment and discretion? What is the question of her ordination-office? 'Will you reverently obey your Bishop and other chief ministers, who, according to the canons of the Church, may have the charge and government over you, following with a glad mind and will their godly admonitions, and submitting yourself to their godly judgments?' And what is the answer of the person ordained? 'I will so do, the Lord being my helper.'"

On this passage the comment of the members is as follows: "The author seems to us to suppose that by this answer the candidate pledges himself, explicitly, to 'obey' his Bishop, to 'follow' his 'admonitions and submit to his judgment.' We have no disposition to with-hold any degree of canonical obedience from our ecclesiastical superior; and, without justly subjecting ourselves to any such charge, must be allowed to maintain, that, in matters not provided for by any legislative act of the Church, each individual must determine for himself whether any particular 'admonition' or 'judgment' is 'godly,' and act accordingly. Let it not be supposed that, by denying such admonition or judgment to be 'godly,' he thereby asserts it to be *ungodly*. It may re-gard an *indifferent* matter, or one in which there is evident room for opposite opinions. 'Every man' must 'be persuaded in *his own mind*.'"

From the view which I have given of the origin and character of the Clerical Associa-tion, of the objections which were brought against it, and of the tenor of the reply, it must be evident that the ground taken by the Bishop would give him an uncontrolled influ-ence, in matters not provided for, either by in-herent Episcopal right or by legitimate authority; and also that the members of the Association were unwilling to succumb to such an unauthorized claim. I do not doubt that the views of the great body of the Episcopal clergy accorded with those of "the Defense." Indeed one of the most respectable presbyters in the Church, who was afterwards advanced to the Episcopate, and has, all his life, been classed with what are called High-Churchmen, understanding that I was preparing a reply to the pastoral, told me that the presbyters in general would come out on our side. But, when the controversy came to its height, they thought it most prudent, with a few exceptions, not to make their sympathies public.

The Account and Defense of the Association were soon followed by a "Brief Notice" of it. The name of the author was not given, but it was generally ascribed to Bishop Hobart. The writer considers the view taken "of the nature of the ordination-vow" one "among the many extraordinary things in the Account." To show how little regard he paid to the right of private judgment in things indifferent, I quote the following passage: "Things are good, bad, or indifferent. Under the two former are classed the things good or bad in themselves, or by divine or human prescription." (This is not very clear, as a question might be raised respecting the right, bearing, and extent of the latter.) "With regard to these, the Bishop can not interfere, except so far as legitimately to enforce their observance, and in cases of doubt to express his judgment. It is to things indifferent that the promise of obedience has principally reference. In regard to these the promise characterizes the admonition and judgment of the Bishop as 'godly,' making that *right, proper, and a matter of duty*, which before was indifferent. To suppose that it permits the individual to determine whether, in matters of indifference, the judgment and admonition of the Bishop be godly or not, is a quibble most unworthy of the sacredness of the subject. It nullifies the promise, makes it words and nothing more." Thus every thing, without any exception, may be rightfully and authoritatively settled for a clergyman, if it shall please his Bishop to give his decision. "Things good or bad" come under the head of "divine prescription," and are, consequently, settled by direct divine law. "Things indifferent" are made "matters of duty" by the expressed "admonition and judgment" of the Bishop. The clergyman's obligation, therefore, is settled for every thing, unless his Bishop declines to interfere! It never seems to have occurred to the writer, that "the admonitions and judgments" of a Bishop are spoken of, in the service, as "godly," on the supposition that they would really be so, and be given only in cases where a truly religious element is involved. No: Episcopal "judgment" "*makes what is indifferent, a duty!*" No wonder that a presbyter, and one whose general theological views and course of action accorded with the Bishop's, remarked in reference to this extravagant claim, that, on such a principle, he might expect obedience, if he should require his clergy to have all their books bound in black!

In this connection the writer of the "Brief Notice" introduces me by name, as "the author of the Account," although its title-page attributes it to "the members of the Association," and I was merely their agent. "He does especially wonder that reasoning which appears to him so palpably sophistical, should deliberately come from the pen of a professor of divinity in the Theological Seminary; for it is no secret that the Rev. Dr. Turner is the author of the 'Account, etc.'" Here he refers directly to the Seminary, and speaks of the mischief which would result from "the students becoming converts to the opinions of the professor." In this connection he adds, also, the following note, the intended bearing of which is evident enough: "It is a curious fact in the history of human nature, in its religious character, that those who make the highest pretensions to evangelical piety, and who therefore ought to excel in the evangelical grace of humility, often display that restlessness under the influence of even lawful authority, that jealousy of superior station, and that extreme solicitude to sink as low as possible its powers, and to yield as little as possible to its claims, which are as inconsistent with the lofty feelings of the high-minded and independent man, as with the lowliness and meekness of the Christian." I never replied to this announcement of my name, and representation of my character. I resolved to live out the odium, without taking notice of the attack, in the hope that the feelings of all concerned would gradually become calmed. I was quite willing to leave those who knew me personally, to form their own judgments as to the applicability of the description. I never to this day have regretted the part I took in the whole affair of the Association, and am still of the opinion that the ground taken in "the Defense" is solid. One of the members, Mr. Seabury, wrote, on his own account, a reply to the pastoral letter, which I was informed was very full, and, to use the author's words, was "a review of the *principles and facts* involved." It was very particular and pointed, especially in reference to the causes which gave occasion to the rise of Methodism. It was not without much persuasion that he could be induced to relinquish the intention of publishing. Dr. Wainwright strongly dissuaded him. I conveyed to him my solicitude on the subject, and my hope that he would not issue a publication, which might contribute to continue excitement; expressing my willingness to bear whatever odium might attach to the authorship of "the Defense." In reply he wrote me a very kind letter, in which he says that " a clergyman and a layman in whose judgment he could confide, while they approved entirely of all that he had written, and were pleased to speak highly of some parts of it, yet strenuously advised him not to publish." He expresses his " most sincere sympathy with me in the treatment I had received." He did "not think the author capable of " writing what he calls, " most ungenerous — more so than he would be if he would leave his mind to its native workings." Of the truth of this last remark I have no doubt. Bishop Hobart's ardent temperament, operating upon what the same writer calls "impracticable principles," and a consciousness that he had often been unjustly represented, as disposed to exert official power unduly, and without proper regard for those who were below him in ecclesiastical position, produced some excitement, and induced him to use language which, both in its general strain and personal application, could not be justified. But his warm and affectionate disposition after a while resumed its natural influence. For a short time a coolness marked our intercourse; but in a few months the whole matter apparently died away. Each of us knew that entire sympathy in all the details of ecclesiastical matters was not to be expected in the other, and avoided the introduction of topics which might tend to collision.

In addition to what I have here written on the subject of "The Clerical Association," I will add that some persons accused its founders of the design of forming an ecclesiastical party, by whose influence in the diocese, Dr. Wainwright might be elected Bishop, either assistant or principal, if any occasion should arise to make an appointment desirable or necessary. I can only say that I never heard the least intimation of such a purpose from any member, that it is very doubtful to me whether he would have been acceptable to some of them, and that so unworthy a motive ought not to have been imputed to clergymen of character and respectability without clear proof. Yet I know this to have been regarded by some as the prominent object of the Association; and more than twenty years after the affair, I heard the statement made by one of the oldest presbyters of Western New-York. Indeed, "the Vindication of the Pastoral Letter" contains a passage which shows that the writer was not without apprehension that this Association, and others also, supposing them to be formed, might exert such an elective influence. "Suppose a *vacancy in the Episcopate of this Diocese* should occur, is it without the range of probability that an event so important and exciting as the election of a Bishop would not be brought under consideration in one or more of these associations?" I do not know who was the author of this Vindication, but it appears to contain internal evidence of proceeding from the pen of the Bishop, or, at least, of having been subjected to his inspection and modification.

In the year 1828, Messrs. Eastburn and

Schroeder, the former of whom was assistant minister of Christ Church, and the latter, one of those connected with Trinity, formed an association with Mr. Whittingham, then Librarian of the Seminary, and myself, for mutual improvement in Biblical Literature. We met once in two weeks, when one of us read a paper, which was subjected to the remarks of the others. In a short time, our critical stock having somewhat accumulated, we resolved to publish a volume, and in 1829 issued from the press of the Carvills, *Essays and Dissertations in Biblical Literature*, octavo, pages 567. With the exception of a Life of Bochart by Mr. Whittingham, the work consisted of translations, the most important of which are those by Mr. Eastburn, of Storrs's Dissertation on the Kingdom of Heaven, from his Opuscula, and Tittmann's Book on Gnosticism.* Mr. Schroeder contributed a translation of Eichhorn on the Authenticity and Canonical Authority of the Scriptures of the Old Testament, and also of a treatise by John David Michaelis on the Study of the Syriac Language. My portion consisted of a brief sketch of the history of Introductions to the Bible, by Gesenius, and also the same author's History of the In-

* De Vestigiis Gnosticorum in N. T. quæ sitis.

terpretation of Isaiah, translated from the In
troduction to his Commentary on that prophet.
Volume I. remains a monument of industrious
enterprise; but it met with no success, and a
second was never ventured.

CHAPTER VIII.

Elected Professor of Hebrew Language in Columbia College—
Lectures in the College Chapel—Their Publication—Discour-
agements—Death of his Daughter—Translation and Publication of Professor Planck's Introduction to Theological
Knowledge, with Notes—Birth of his first Son—Peter G.
Stuyvesant's Endowment of a Professorship in the Seminary—Death of Mrs. Turner—Publication of "Companion to
the Book of Genesis"—Object of the Work—Criticisms of two
Church Papers.

THE monotonous tenor of my life, for several
subsequent years, affords but little worthy of
notice. In 1830, while efforts were in progress
to establish the New-York University, Columbia College thought it expedient to revive her
old professorship of Hebrew, which many
years before had been held by the Rev. Dr.
Kuntze, whom I have had occasion to mention,
and which had continued vacant since his
death. Very much to my surprise, the choice
fell on me, and since that time I have enjoyed
the title of "Professor of the Hebrew Language and Literature in Columbia College."
In order to bring the subject of the Professorship somewhat before the public, I delivered,
in 1831, three lectures in the Chapel of the
College. They were afterwards printed in the

8

Biblical Repository, Vol. I. No. III. pages 491–530, Andover, 1831, under the title, *Claims of the Hebrew Language and Literature*. They excited very little interest however, and I doubt whether the number of the auditors amounted to thirty on any one occasion, although the lectures were free to all. Scarcely any of the clergy attended; but Bishop Hobart was regularly present. It was my original intention to continue the course, but I abandoned it for want of encouragement. During two or three winters I gave gratuitous instruction to small classes every Saturday at the Seminary. The first class consisted of Messrs. Richard Cox, Anthony Ten Broeck, and James A. Williams, all of whom afterwards became students of the Seminary and clergymen of our Church. At the termination of their attendance, they kindly presented me with a copy of an edition of the Septuagint and Greek Testament in three very neat volumes in eighteenmo, with the inscription: "To Dr. Samuel H. Turner, from his first Hebrew Class in Columbia College, June 22, 1833." As pocket-volumes, I have found the work very convenient. After a while, however, when Nordheimer became known as a good Hebrew teacher, I felt it the less incumbent on me to devote my time to this object. Since then I have never been required to give lessons in Hebrew, so that the professorship has become a sinecure.

On Saturday, March sixteenth, 1833, our daughter Cornelia, whom, we had fondly hoped, God had given us as a substitute for our beloved Julia, was attacked with inflammation of the chest, and on the following Wednesday, the twentieth, went to join those spirits whose "angels do always behold the face of the Father." She was a very sweet and lovely child, wanting two days of being eighteen months old. Her loss, which left us with but one remaining daughter, was too deeply felt, both by her mother and myself, to be expressed.

At several biblical meetings with the three clergymen before mentioned, I had read portions of a translation which I had made from a German work entitled *Introduction to Theological Knowledge*, by Dr. G. J. Planck, Professor of Theology at Göttingen. The parts of this work which I had selected were those which treated of sacred criticism and interpretation. I was thus led to prepare the translation for publication. I appended a considerable amount of notes, one of which comprehended an analysis, though indeed brief, of

Griesbach's Prolegomena, and an explanation
of his critical marks. The work was published by Leavitt and Company in 1834, in
duodecimo, pages 306. The edition was limited
to seven hundred and fifty copies, of which
about thirty-five were sold. The book was republished in Edinburgh as the fourth volume
of the Biblical Cabinet. With the exception
of about seventy, twenty of which I placed in
the library of the Seminary for the use of students, I gave the whole edition away to successive classes.

I have nothing of any interest to relate until
the birth of my first son, which took place at
Cheshire, Connecticut, in the house of his
grandfather, on the third of August, 1835.
This was an occasion of great joy and thankfulness. He was baptized in St. Peter's Church,
in the village, by the rector, the Rev. E. E.
Beardsley, and was called Herbert Beach. The
name was chosen on account of its similarity
to my own, (after my father's uncle,) Hulbeart,
and its identity with that of the good country
parson, George Herbert, whom I then prayed
God that my child might resemble in devotion
and piety.

As the funds of the Seminary had become
considerably enlarged, the Trustees determined

to erect another building on the western part of the ground. It was to correspond with the former in its general aspect and construction, although it was to be a few feet longer, and thus to enlarge a little the students' rooms, making each more convenient for the accommodation of two. Arrangements were also made for better ventilation. The east end was to be prepared as a house for one of the professors, and, as the choice was mine, I determined to make it my future residence. Not liking the construction and arrangement of the house in the older building, I endeavored to secure an improvement. With a view to this, I made an offer, through Professor McVickar, to the building committee, which was partly agreed to, and thereby the construction of the house became greatly superior to that of the other two. In the spring of 1836 I moved into it, and have resided there ever since.

At a stated meeting of the Trustees, held August fourteenth, 1835, Mr. Peter G. Stuyvesant made an offer of twenty-five thousand dollars, to found a professorship, on the condition of his being allowed to nominate the professor, subject to the approbation of the Trustees. The generous offer was gratefully accepted, and Mr. Stuyvesant, on the twenty-first of September, 1835, nominated "the Rev. Francis L. Hawks, D.D., Rector of St. Thomas's Church in the city of New-York, as Professor of the 'St. Mark's in the Bowery,' Professorship of Ecclesiastical History." Afterwards, however, at a special meeting held November twenty-fifth, of the same year, "Dr. Hawks having previously declined the nomination," "The Rev. William R. Whittingham, a presbyter of the diocese of New-York," was substituted. At the same meeting a communication was received from South-Carolina, signed by the Bishop and four other clergymen, proposing as professor in the same department the Rev. Samuel F. Jarvis, D.D. At a special meeting, held January thirteenth, 1836, called for the purpose of acting on Mr. Stuyvesant's nomination, it was unanimously approved of, and Mr. Whittingham was declared to be the professor. He immediately entered upon his duties, retaining also the office of librarian, to which he had been before appointed, and appropriating either the whole or a large part of the salary of one hundred dollars to some student who assisted him in discharging the duties of the office. A few years after, Mr. Whittingham was elected Bishop of the Church in Maryland, and, after his consecration to the office, he resigned his professorship on November first, 1840, and the next day Mr. Stuyvesant nominated as his successor "the Rev John D. Ogilby, Professor of Ancient Languages in Rutgers College, in the State of New-Jersey, and a presbyter of the diocese." A special meeting was held on the second of December in the same year, when the nomination was unanimously approved of, and Mr. Ogilby became professor.

At the triennial meeting of the Board, held October fourteenth, 1841, "the Rev. Benjamin I. Haight, a presbyter of the diocese of New-York, was duly nominated by a vote of the Board to the Professorship of Pastoral Theology and Pulpit Eloquence;" and at a special meeting held on the thirtieth of the following November, the nomination was unanimously approved. On the third of December, 1841, Mr. Haight accepted the professorship. He was at the same time rector of All Saints' Church, and continued to retain this position. In June, 1842, the mode of conducting commencements was altered. The reading of dissertations by the Senior class was dispensed with, and the present arrangement adopted.

I have, for the sake of convenience, thrown together the previously mentioned matters relating to the Seminary. I must now go back to the most melancholy event which marks my domestic life.

It had been our usual custom to spend most of the summer vacations with my father-in-law and his daughters at Cheshire. There we enjoyed ourselves with pleasant rural scenes and social gratifications. I always pursued some regular course of Hebrew or German study, and of general reading, and, on occasions of a temporary vacancy in the parish, supplied the church, and, when there was a rector, assisted him, and sometimes other clergymen in the neighboring towns, in the duties of the desk and pulpit. Thus the vacations were passed very agreeably, and I hope usefully; and the pure country air was conducive to our physical health. In the season of 1839 it was thought best to remain at home, and we spent but a few days in Connecticut. Early in August my dear wife was attacked with dysentery, and, after a course of severe suffering from the disease, she gave birth to a second son on the fourteenth. He was baptized on the third of September at home by the Rev. Hugh Smith, D.D., Rector of St. Peter's, and named Joseph, after my father and brother, and Mason after the latter and my mother. The child's mother, alas! did not stand as a sponsor, her place being supplied by my sister Eliza. She had gone to join " the spirits of the just made perfect." The very severe attack of that painful disease was too much even for her strong constitution to bear up under, and on the second of September her soul left its earthly tenement, and winged its course to that better world, where sickness and pain and sorrow are alike unknown. Some days before her death, she had become apparently better; and I could not but feel encouraged to cherish the faint and lingering hope which I had indulged, that my earnest prayers might be answered, and that she might yet recover to bless my declining years with the many satisfactions arising from her presence, and to aid me in bringing up our children in the nurture and admonition of the Lord. But *Deo aliter visum.* What I then felt and thought I shall not attempt to describe. A little of this you may find in the memorandum inserted in the Bible before mentioned. But the feeling has grown with the growth of years and become habitual, and although I have tried hard to be resigned to the will of God, knowing from reasonable faith that it is wise and good, and even merciful, yet unable to see by my weak understanding the full reason for her removal,

8*

ever since her death I have felt alone in
the world, though surrrounded by the kindest
friends, and blessed with the most attentive
relatives and children. She is gone with whom
I was united in heart and soul, with whom I
had lived more than thirteen years in harmony
and love, uninterrupted by one unkind word or
feeling. Her departure has left a void which
neither time nor the respect and affection of
others can fill. She was most highly respected and dearly beloved by all who were well
acquainted with her; and although you never
can fully know the loss you have sustained by
her death, you may be able somewhat to ap-
preciate the character of your mother, from the
estimate in which her memory is held by those
who knew her best. Truly God's "judgments
are unsearchable, and his ways past finding
out." The remains of my beloved wife were
deposited in a vault in St. Mark's church-yard.
In a few months I had these, along with those
of our two children, removed to her family
burial-ground at Cheshire. In my last will
and testament, I have directed my own to be
placed in the same consecrated ground, in the
hope of a joyous resurrection.

After I had partially recovered from the
overwhelming shock occasioned by my heavy

domestic calamity, I resolved to endeavor to devote my leisure time to some useful employment connected with my position in the Seminary. I therefore began to revise some notes on the book of Genesis which I had written in an interleaved copy of Michaelis's Hebrew Bible, and had used in lectures to the students. A thorough revision was necessary, and the whole matter had to be examined and written anew, and many additional sources of information investigated and compared. The result was embodied in a work entitled *Companion to the Book of Genesis*, which was published in the spring of 1841, by Wiley and Putnam, octavo, pages 405. It consisted of an analysis of this first book of the Pentateuch, and a commentary which, on the more important portions, was considerably extended, the divisions in both being into sections, according to the respective subjects. An introduction of sixty-six pages discusses the documentary theory and other matters of interest and importance.

The treatment which this publication received from two of our Church papers was remarkable. In my remarks on the account of the fall, in the third chapter of Genesis, and particularly on the agent in the temptation, I had

stated at some length the three prominent
views. On the second and third I had declined expressing positive opinion respecting
the point whether the tempter, whom I considered as identical with the devil, employed
as his instrument the animal called serpent,
or whether this form of reptile was designed
to express allegorically the cunning and insid-
ious nature of the tempter. In either view,
the reality of the facts of the temptation and
the fall remained unaffected. I had expressed
the opinion that the paradisiacal trees were to
be understood literally, and that the prohibi-
tion of the fruit of one of them was intended
to try and improve the character of our first
parents. In a periodical then in course of publication at Flushing, an article appeared, in
which the writer attempted to amuse his readers by speaking of the girls' samplers in former years, on which it was the fashion to de-
lineate pictures of the narrative by working
serpents with apples in their mouths. This specimen of what looks like the littleness of infidel sneering, was published in a Church periodical! The writer intended, of course, to
ridicule my silly superstition.

A short time before the publication of this
article, an editorial notice of my book appear-

ed in a Church paper published in this city. While Mr. Whittingham was a professor in the Seminary, a difficulty had arisen between him and the editor, occasioned by some remarks on a former editorial, entitled: "On the Salvability of the Heathen." These remarks were printed in a Philadelphia Church paper, contrary to the intention of the writer, who had marked them *private*. As the editor of this latter paper had introduced them as coming from the Seminary, the resident professors were treated by the New-York periodical in no very courteous way. For a time, Dr. Wilson and myself declined taking any part in the discussion. After the appearance, however, of several articles, one or two of which bore the signature of "A Trustee," we sent a communication, stating that we had no connection with the remarks which had appeared in the Philadelphia paper, and showing to what extent we had expressed our opinions on the original article. As I had gone somewhat beyond Dr. Wilson in this point, I laid myself the more open, as opportunity should arise, to animadversion and censure. Consequently, when my book appeared, it was attacked extravagantly, and with utter want of that discrimination which might have been reasonably expected. An uninformed reader would naturally have supposed that I had written something tending to subvert the authority of revealed religion. The following citation is sufficient: "We do not question the *right* of any man to despise the consent of the Fathers, and spend his life in balancing the conflicting opinions of modern critics in matters on which the Fathers are agreed; nor do we question his *right* to deny the Nicene faith; nor, in fine, his *right* to abjure the Christian religion and to advocate infidelity." Was ever any thing more extraordinary! Not to recognize *consent* of the Fathers on multitudes of points on which *they differ* from each other nearly as much as modern writers, is, with some, almost a species of infidelity. It were well if such persons would take the trouble of ascertaining in what matters the Fathers are agreed, and in what they vary from each other. But they ignore the principle involved in the divine words: "We speak that we do know, and testify that we have seen."

The portion of my book to which particular reference is made, is the very same which had been contemptuously objected to in the Flushing paper as bordering on the superstitious and the silly. In the view of the New-York writer, it presented evidence of neology. In a pam-

phlet which I found necessary, in 1845, to publish in my own defense, I introduced this remark in reference to the opposite views of superstition and neology entertained by the two
writers alluded to : "To be dashed on the rocks
of Scylla by the one, and consigned by the
other to the gulf of Charybdis, is hard. Perhaps the reader who is not altogether under
the influence of that literary autocracy which
is apt to show itself in all sorts of periodicals,
may be inclined to think that the author has
steered his bark sufficiently in the middle of
the dangerous strait to avoid the mischief
threatened from both sides."

This pamphlet, which I introduced with a
motto taken from the first line of Juvenal, as
being particularly appropriate to the repeated
attacks, direct and indirect, upon me, which
thus far I had passed over without reply, was
not answered nor in any way noticed by the
periodical. I have introduced the matter here,
merely because of its intimate and *necessary*
connection with the narrative relating to the
Seminary, and the action of the Trustees and
the House of Bishops; of all which, I shall
now give a brief account.

CHAPTER IX.

History of the Seminary—New-York City an Unfavorable Location—Effects of the Doctrines of the Oxford Tracts and their kindred Usages — Conflicting Views with regard to them — Suggestion of the Examining Committee — Dissent of Drs. Anthon and Smith, in the Committee — Professor Turner's Reply to the Implied Censure—The true Place and Value of the Early Fathers in the Exposition of Scripture—A Proposition to the Trustees—Resolutions of the South-Carolina Convention — Unfavorable Rumors in regard to the Seminary—Report of the South-Carolina Committee—Singular Questions propounded to the Faculty—Episcopal Visitation of the Seminary — Professor Turner's Answers — Communication from Bishop McIlvaine—Christmas Novelties—Apostasies to Rome — Professor Turner's Resistance to Novelties — The Attempt of "The Churchman" to Ridicule his Published Statement of Facts—"Records of Councils"—Its Ignorance and Indecency —Resolutions of the Visiting-Bishops — The Real Value of their Opinion—Romanism among the Students—Secret Plans for Propagating it—Action of the Faculty—Expulsions from the Seminary—The Expelled Students Ordained in New-York, North-Carolina and Maryland — Further Apostasies to Rome —Influences Outside of the Seminary—The Errors and Cant Phrases of the Times — Characters most easily led astray — The Responsibility of those who Recommend Candidates for Orders — Resignation of Professors Wilson and Moore—Professor Ogilby's Death — Appointment of Professor Johnson and Mahan.

THE principal object which I have in view in preparing this sketch requires me to revert again to matters connected with the Seminary.

The Institution had been conducted with as much success as could reasonably be expected, taking into consideration its position and connections. I have no hesitation in saying that its reëstablishment in the city of New-York always appeared objectionable to me, though I do not think it expedient to state my reasons in detail. It was removed here from New-Haven, and became a respectable and useful school of theological instruction. The number of its pupils gradually increased, until from twenty-four, the total amount of the three classes in 1825, it reached, in eleven years, its climax of eighty-seven. It continued for a long time to retain respectable numbers, averaging about seventy-three or seventy-four. The course of instruction and the action of the professors were approved of, and the examinations were reported as highly respectable. But the introduction into the Church of the Oxford Tracts, with the ultra views which, in some minds, they either originated or confirmed, and extended in others, and the determined opposition to them which sprang up among those of moderate and Low-Church principles, had its influence on trustees, professors, and students. The desire to eliminate the word *Protestant* from our Prayer-Book and other Church authorities, and to substitute *Reformed Catholic*;

the disposition to multiply outward religious services, and to perform them with peculiar ceremonies not before used in our Church, including also the chanting of the Psalter, which became much more common than formerly; the increased fondness for crosses, plain or extravagantly ornamented; the eagerness to appeal to the fathers, as the legitimate test of true doctrine and exposition, and even by men who could not read a sentence in the original; all showed a growing tendency, to append to what had heretofore been regarded as the true rule of faith, and a sufficient exhibition of sound devotion, excrescences, which the body of wise and judicious men had generally regarded, not only as unnecessary, but practically injurious. The existence in various degrees of such a feeling, and the consequent reäction it naturally produced, are necessary to be kept in view, in forming a right judgment of the movements now to be referred to.

The first intimation I have found of any thing like an inclination to censure, growing out of the feeling above mentioned, appears in the Report of the Examining Committee for 1843. In reference to my examination of the Middle class on some of the Epistles, they "suggest that attention be particularly paid to the early fathers of the Church, both as witnesses of how the sacred Scriptures of the New Testament were understood by those to whom they were first committed, and as also themselves well fitted, from their character, position, and other circumstances, to be useful aids to interpretation." One of the members of this committee afterwards became a pervert to the Romanists. Two others, Drs. Anthon and Smith, "dissented from this portion of the Report, on the ground that "it contained, in their judgment, an incorrect view of the true authority of the fathers, no distinct statement of who are the early fathers, and seemed to them unjust to the professor in that department, from their experience of his perfect fidelity."

At the next meeting, held in June, 1844, the Faculty added to their general report a special communication, under my signature. In it I requested "directions from the Trustees in reference to a portion of the last Annual Report," just quoted. I expressed my "regret that the Committee should have thought it their duty to incorporate this 'suggestion' in a report made to the Trustees, and according to ordinary usage intended for publication, without any previous conference with the professor, whose supposed omission appears to be thereby censured." I went on to say that "a suitable measure of attention to the early fathers" had been paid; that "an examination of them in reference to the interpretation of Scripture, in order to be conducted usefully, would require a degree of learning and a faculty of discrimination, which young men, entering on a course of divinity, can not in general be supposed to possess." I stated my willingness, if the Trustees would "so direct, to devote a part of the time now employed in explaining the sacred Scriptures, to a course of lectures on the principles and method of exposition of the early fathers;" I referred, however, to the extensiveness of the subject, and the very limited time "appropriated to the department of Biblical Learning and the Interpretation of Scripture," which, "during the entire period" of the course, did "not exceed one hundred and twenty-five" full days. "Whether it be expedient to take a single day from this comparatively small amount of time now employed in the direct critical and exegetical study of the Scriptures, in order to devote it to the early history of Interpretation, the Trustees, in their wisdom, will decide." To this communication no reply was made. The report, presented at the same meeting, of the Committee, who attended the intermediate examination, then held in the month of February, contains also another expressive hint, in the words following: "In the exegesis of the sacred text, great attention should be paid to the numerous false interpretations which have been given. The student who is preparing for the ministry of the Church ought to be familiarly acquainted with all the phases of error. This is well; but at the same time it would seem to be all-important that he should not be left to the exercise of his own private judgment as to what *the truth is*. The Church professes to teach catholic doctrine. This should be the standard by which all human opinions must be tried: the sooner the student is put in possession of, and taught to apply this standard, the better." Thus the doctrine of the Church of England, that the Scriptures are the sole rule of faith, was set aside, and "the Church," or its "catholic doctrine," substituted in its place. The nature of the examination and instruction alluded to, may be inferred from this language of the Committee, which consisted of only three members. (See Proceedings, page 402.) A few years afterwards one of them joined the Church of Rome.

At the same meeting certain resolutions, passed by the Convention of South-Carolina, having a reference to some rumors unfavorable to the Seminary, were laid before the Board. They were referred to a committee, "to report in the fullest manner" at the ensuing triennial meeting, which was held on the thirtieth of September following. The Rev. Mr. Trapier of South-Carolina, a member of the committee, made a report containing a full statement of their proceedings, which had been conducted, partly at meetings held in June during the annual session of the Board, and partly during an adjourned meeting held in the latter part of September. The rumors related to instructions said to have been given respecting the practice of infant communion in the primitive Church, and the heretical character of the Church of Rome. The statements, and extracts of letters containing them, were ordered to be entered on the minutes, and may be found on pages 419, 420. The report contains also certain questions or "heads of inquiry proposed to the professors," together with the answers thereto. The last question would not have come with much consistency from those Trustees whose names are appended to the report, just referred to, of the intermediate examination. It runs thus: "Do the teachings of the professors inculcate that holy Scripture is the supreme rule of faith, as is taught in the sixth article of the thirty-nine?" The concluding paragraph of "the Draft of the Report of the Board of Trustees to the General Convention," contained the following: "The Trustees feel assured that the General Theological Seminary has never been in a more healthful condition than it is at the present time." These words, "the Rev. Mr. Trapier moved to strike out." The motion was sustained by a vote of twenty-five, including Bishops Brownell, Hopkins, McIlvaine, Kemper, and Eastburn. It was negatived by a vote of twenty-six members, among whom were Bishops Onderdonk, Doane, Ives, and Gadsden. "Bishop McIlvaine then moved that the Secretary be ordered to lay before the House of Bishops all the documents connected with the proceedings of the Committee on the resolutions of the South-Carolina Convention, which have been read to this Board,—and the same was negatived." (See the Proceedings of The Stated Triennial Meeting, page 442.) The unwillingness of a majority of the Board to lay open before the official visitors all the circumstances connected with the "rumors unfavorable to the Seminary," is evident. It is not, therefore, to be wondered at, that a minority presented to the following General Convention "a brief statement," containing the expression of "their dissent from the said report." This was signed by Bishops Hopkins, McIlvaine, and Eastburn, by the Rev. Dr. Anthon, and Messrs. Barnwell and Neufville, and by Mr. P. G. Stuyvesant.

If the statements just made are duly considered, it will not appear at all surprising that, immediately on the assembling of the House of Bishops at the next General Convention held in Philadelphia, early in October, Bishop Chase presiding, the state of the Seminary was brought up for consideration. As they were officially visitors of the Institution, "to see that the instruction and discipline be duly carried out," it became their duty to exercise their legitimate authority. A set of forty questions was therefore prepared by them, a copy of which was transmitted to each of the professors, with three additional ones addressed exclusively to the Professor of Ecclesiastical History, "requesting answers at their earliest convenience." I never was more amazed than when reading some of these questions, and occasionally the thought occurred to me that the document could not be genuine. Some of the questions appeared irrelevant; others to imply what was wholly improbable; others, again, to have been proposed simply in order to counterbalance what had been previously admitted, so that one class might neutralize the other. I was hardly able to persuade myself that they could have originated with such a body. The following language was used of them in the *Churchman*, not long after the visitation, which took place immediately after the Convention: "If the Pope, the Oxford Tracts, the father of modern neology, and Calvinism had been present in person or in effigy; and if the questions had been elicited from the Right Rev. Fathers by their several fears of each, and had then been shaken in a hat, and drawn out for numerical arrangement, they could not have had less coherence and mutual dependence." I will quote a few, in illustration of what I have said, without having the least knowledge of the individual Bishops who suggested them:

"11. Are the works of Toplady, of Thomas Scott, and John Newton, and Blunt on the Articles, or any of them, used as text-books, or publicly or privately recommended to the students of the Seminary?" It is not to be supposed that any member of the House of Bishops could have thought that Dr. Wilson, the professor under whose supervision the topics

9

alluded to would properly come, was likely to use such books; and certainly no other professor could have been intended. The next question solves the phenomenon: "12. Are the works of the Rev. Dr. Pusey, Messrs. Newman, Keble, Palmer, Ward, and Massingberd, or any of them, used as text-books, or publicly or privately recommended in the Seminary?" Massingberd had been used for a short time, though entirely unworthy of such a distinction. It had never been adopted as a text-book. The one question is evidently a set-off to the other. So also the 28th 29th, and 30th in contradistinction to the 31st and 32d: "Are the Oxford Tracts adopted as text-books in the Seminary? Are they publicly or privately recommended to the students? Is Tract 90 used as a text-book, or (so) recommended?" On the other side: "Is Calvinism, comprehending what are known as the 'five points,' (so) taught or recommended? Is any one of the five points (so) taught or recommended?" Again: "41. What has the Professor of Ecclesiastical History taught concerning the heretical character of the Roman Church? 42. Concerning the Constantinopolitan creed?" These are followed by: "43. Is the doctrine of 'limited atonement,' and of 'reprobation,' taught in the Seminary?" I do not believe that any member of the House of Bishops had the least idea that such doctrines were taught. Once more: " 36. Are the superstitious practices of the Romish Church, such as the use or worship of the crucifix, of images of saints, and the invocation of the blessed Virgin, and other saints, adopted, or publicly or privately recommended in the Seminary?" To outweigh which, follows: " 37. Is the German system of rationalism—that is, of rejecting every thing mysterious in the doctrines and institutions of the Gospel, and making human reason the sole umpire in theology, adopted, or (so) recommended in the Seminary? 38. Are German, or other authors who support that system, adopted as text-books, or (so) recommended as guides of theological opinion?" As disclosing the same feeling which gave rise to these two questions, I add the 14th : " Has it been publicly or privately taught in the Seminary, that any portion of the sacred narrative in the book of Genesis is in the nature of a myth, or is merely or principally allegorical?" Subsequently I mentioned to one of the Right Reverend gentlemen who had proposed some similarly objectionable questions to the Committee of the Board of Trustees, my impression that certain of the Bishops' questions were introduced just to stand in contra-distinction to certain others; and his reply was—"EXACTLY so!" The inquiries last cited evidently refer to what had been ungenerously and untruly stated in reference to my comment, in the *Companion to Genesis*, on the fall of man.

It will be sufficient for me to give the substance of some of the answers in my own communication. To state those of the other professors does not come within my purpose. To the 14th, just cited, I replied as follows: "Not to my knowledge. So far as relates to myself, very particular pains have been taken to show the fallacy of the system referred to; and this I have also done in my *Companion to the Book of Genesis*." My answer to the 37th and 38th was designedly full. I intended it to comprehend a reply to the charge of rationalistic tendency which had been advanced after the publication of the volume before mentioned, and which seemed to give shape and character to the two questions. I shall transcribe it in full: "Presuming that these questions are intended to bear principally on my department, the Bishops will pardon me if I express my great surprise that they should have been proposed. If there be any one thing for which I feel conscious that I merit the approval of the Trustees and the Church, it is for the uniform opposition which I have made to the whole system referred to, whether appearing in Germany, England, or America. The book before mentioned, (in the reply to the 14th question,) contains satisfactory evidence of this, and exposes some matters in the Hebrew Lexicon of Gesenius, even where the student could hardly suppose a rationalistic tendency to show itself. The Introduction to the Old Testament, (Jahn's,) published several years ago by one of your Right Reverend body and myself, though it is very far from being what I could wish, abounds with similar proofs; and, indeed, the Rev. Dr. Horne incorporated a portion of it with his own Introduction *for this very reason*, and wrote to me on the subject, at the same time presenting me with a copy of his work *as an acknowledgment*. In my instruction to the classes, I have particularly guarded them against the whole theory of rationalism, most especially as regards the interpretation of prophecy and miracles, considering it as neither more nor less than disguised infidelity. With such views of it, I of course reply to the questions very decidedly in the negative."

In addition to this most extraordinary collection of questions proposed by the House of Bishops, I received a communication from Bishop McIlvaine, to understand the purport of which it is necessary to mention a matter which might under other circumstances properly be passed over. It is trifling in itself, but as indicating a state of feeling in the minds of some students, and as remarked upon by one of our Church papers, and noted in an English publication, it assumes a degree of importance which otherwise could not attach to it.

The day before Christmas, 1843, I happened to go into the long-room, which was used as a Chapel, to see how it was dressed. My attention was arrested by a wooden cross, about two feet high, placed on the front railing of the chancel, ornamented partly by evergreens, and partly by artificial flowers. As rumors of certain practices accordant with those of the Church of Rome being in use by some students, had already been considerably circulated, and in very exaggerated forms; and as one student, who in all probability entered with Romanist tendencies, had lately left the Seminary and joined that Church, I thought it highly inexpedient to suffer a novelty like this to pass unnoticed. I considered also, that, as the Seminary was an institution of the whole Protestant Episcopal Church in the United States, it would be wrong to allow what would reasonably be regarded as objectionable by a large proportion of that body; and believing, moreover, that the axiom *obsta principiis* was particularly applicable in the present instance, the next day, I required the cross to be removed, thereby exercising a power which I believed to be vested in the Dean, by the statutes. The same night, Christmas-eve, the Seminary - bell was rung at twelve o'clock, to the surprise and annoyance of the neighborhood; and some of the students, without asking permission of the Dean or Faculty, held a midnight service in the Chapel. I was afterwards told that they had placed a paper representation of an illuminated star at one end of the room, and that in the course of the service it got on fire, and had to be taken hastily to the basement, to prevent mischief. In the same note which directed the removal of the cross, I stated my objections to the midnight service, and mentioned the entering into the Chapel not by the door, the key of which, by a mere chance, happened that night to be in my possession. I think it proper to add that three of the students, then belonging to the Seminary, afterwards connected themselves with the Church of Rome.

I gave Bishop McIlvaine an exact account of this matter in my reply, and consequently it became public. A Church paper made it a topic of contemptuous ridicule, taking a one-sided view, without attributing any weight to the feeling and tendency which it betrayed. And in the year 1846 a work was published in London under the title, *Records of Councils*, which refers to the General Convention of 1844 as the "Council of Philadelphia"! In a note, the writer remarks on this affair in such a very slighting way as to show plainly the tenor of his own ecclesiastical views. He speaks of "an amusing case being brought before the Synod. It seems that the Dean of the Faculty for the year, one Samuel H. Turner, had been *much scandalized* by the sight of a wooden cross, about two feet high, decorated with flowers and evergreens on the chancel-rails of the Chapel. This, *I understand, is not an uncommon custom in the churches of the United States;* but Mr. Turner, it seems, preferred to connect the observation of the pious custom, in this particular case, with the Popish feelings and predilections which *he imagined* to be then rife in the Seminary."

(Page 487.) The general accuracy of the work may be judged of by those who are acquainted with the facts of this case, thus caricatured. The author of the *Record*, who regarded the "charge of Popish views and practices having been favored, as *absurd*," was utterly ignorant of what he undertook to express an opinion upon. In his Preface he acknowledges his obligation to some clergymen•in this country for *information respecting the state of the Church !*

After the replies of the several professors to the Episcopal inquiries had been considered, the House of Bishops held a meeting on the thirtieth of October, at the Seminary. On this occasion an additional portion of correspondence was brought forward and acted on. The next day a second meeting was held; and after Morning Prayer in the Chapel, certain resolutions were adopted, and "the House, after engaging in devotional exercises, conducted by the presiding Bishop, adjourned *sine die.*" Two of the resolutions are as follows:

"*Resolved*, That the Bishops, and visitors, having visited the Seminary and inspected the same, do not find in any of its interior arrangements any evidences that superstitious or Romish practices are allowed or encouraged in the Institution.

9*

" *Resolved*, That the Bishops deem the publication of the questions of the Bishops and the answers of the professors the most appropriate reply to the current rumors respecting the doctrinal teaching of the Seminary."

With regard to the latter, I am compelled to say, that such questions, with the answers which they would naturally produce, appear to me to afford a very *insufficient* reply to the rumors alluded to. Such an investigation was quite inadequate. As to the former, I never heard of the private rooms of the students having been inspected by the Right Reverend visitors. I presume, therefore, that the "interior arrangements" mentioned, relate to those of the Chapel, Library, and Lecture-rooms. A short time after the "Episcopal visitation," I heard, from a source to be entirely relied on, of its having been said by one student, that "if they had come into his room he could have shown them a crucifix." It will be evident from what is yet to be narrated in this connection, that the inquiries and the visitation were practically of little or no benefit. And indeed this might have been expected from the character of both.

The Episcopal visitation was made in October, 1844. About two months and a half afterwards, suspicions fell on some students, not only of Romish tendencies and views, but also of having made direct efforts to propagate these among their fellow-pupils. A brief notice of the matter is necessary, in order to present a correct view of the state of the Seminary at this time. I shall give it, as far as practicable, in the statement made by the Faculty, in reply to a resolution communicated to them by the Trustees, at their annual meeting, in June, 1845, requesting information in reference to discipline, which had been exercised on certain of the students referred to. Dr. Wilson, who was then Dean, drew it up; and this is sufficient warrant for its accuracy. (See Proceedings, page 439, *et seq.*)

"In consequence of voluntary information communicated by several students to Professor Ogilby, he presented on the 23d of December, 1844, distinct charges against —— and —— individually. On these charges trials took place on the seventh of January, 1845; and the witnesses produced were examined, and the parties heard. The Faculty then adjourned until the afternoon of the following day, when a decision was intended to be given. But in consequence of intimations from several students on the morning of that day, that much more evidence existed than had been produced on those trials, and also from the tenor of some of the testimony which had been given, it was deemed proper to pursue the inquiries farther; and to request the students (except the supposed parties concerned) to give to the Faculty such information as they possessed and could communicate. A general inquiry was accordingly commenced into the state of the Seminary in reference to the subjects of complaint, and was continued until the 13th of January, (Sunday excepted,) when the whole evidence was completed."

In the course of the investigation some evidence appeared of a designed coöperation on the part of certain students to effect the above-mentioned purpose. On this point, however, the Faculty were divided in opinion, although the majority regarded it as sufficiently sustained. To my mind much of the evidence adduced coïncided with this view of the case. Still I thought that the facts attested might be explained on the ground of occasional unexpected coïncidence, without resorting to a supposition, which every member of the Faculty would have felt relieved by being able to reject. In resolving on the exercise of discipline the Faculty did not act "on the ground of

theological error simply. They considered the
cases only as the conduct of the parties affect-
ed the relation in which they stood as students in the Seminary, and not as candidates
or orders; in which character they were subject only to the ecclesiastical authority of the
proper diocese. The principle on which the
Faculty proceeded was, that the students charged acted contrary to their duties and engagements to the Institution; that they not merely
themselves embraced theological errors, but
promulgated and maintained them within the
Seminary; that they held themselves, and in-
stilled into the minds of other students, principles of a theological system adverse to that
of our Church, and to the course of instruction
prescribed by the House of Bishops and the
Trustees of the Seminary; that they thus pre-
possessed their own minds and those of others
with error before they could in the regular
course of study engage in the proper examination of those controverted principles, thereby
greatly diminishing the full benefit of that
course to themselves and others; that this conduct tended to create parties among the students with excitement of feeling, thus disturb-
ing the harmony of the Seminary—an effect
which had, in fact, been in part produced, and

threatened to increase, unless a check was applied; that it exposed the Institution itself to the imputation of maintaining and instilling erroneous doctrines and encouraging superstitious practices, and thus injured its reputation and usefulness; that there was danger of its opening a way to extraneous influence through their instrumentality." These were the reasons which governed the Faculty.

The direct result of the investigation was as follows: "On the thirteenth of January, 1845, the Faculty resolved that —— and ——, both of the Middle class, cease to be members of the Seminary, and that they be directed to withdraw from the Institution." I was in favor of a sentence of suspension during the pleasure of the Faculty. I preferred this decision to that of entire separation, because I thought it would afford the persons concerned an opportunity of showing regret for the course they had pursued, and of an endeavor to produce among their brethren a suitable reäction in favor of evangelical truth. The other two students against whom charges had been made were subjected to admonition. This was administered with suitable brevity and characteristic mildness by the Dean.

A week after the admonition had been given,

one of the two withdrew from the Seminary, and sent a letter to the Dean and Faculty stating his reasons for so doing, which were as follows: 1. Because the Faculty had shown disregard to the rights of candidates; 2. Because by remaining he would appear to acquiesce in the justice of the sentence; 3. Because the grounds taken by the Faculty deprive him of reasonable liberty of volition and freedom of discussion; 4. Because the means adopted by the Faculty to obtain evidence are in his opinion unworthy and dishonorable; to which he added other considerations reflecting on that body with pointed injustice. This communication, under the name of the student, was published in the *Churchman*. The letter and its publication show the young man's want of proper respect for his elders in years and superiors in authority. And yet I must do him the justice to say that his usual behavior manifested a kind, gentlemanly and Christian deportment, such as the circle of society in which he had been accustomed to move, and the edution which he had received, might have led one to expect. After some time he was ordained in Brooklyn. He was in delicate health, and survived only a few years. One of the students, whose connection with the Seminary had been severed, afterwards removed to North-Carolina, where he was ordained. The other, who had merely been admonished, continued a member of the Institution until April, when, his health not being good, he withdrew to Connecticut. Subsequently he was ordained there. The other student who was obliged to leave was a candidate in Delaware. His Bishop wrote to me for a copy of the notes I had taken of the late investigation. This request I declined complying with, as the Faculty had agreed not to give publicity to the evidence. I offered him, however, a copy of that particular portion which concerned his own candidate. On examining it, he immediately excluded him from his list. Soon afterwards the young man removed to Maryland, where in due time he became a candidate again, was ordained, and settled in the diocese.

The evidence showed, that there were students whose views in some points were Romish, and whose intention was, after entering upon parochial duties within our Church, to endeavor gradually to lead their congregations along with themselves to the Church of Rome. Wild and fanatical project, with which it were absurd to imagine that the people could have been made to coöperate! Yet so deeply had unsound, jesuitical principles insinuated themselves into the mind, in defiance of morality and common-sense. There is good reason to believe that the principles and tendency were, in *most* cases, brought into the Seminary by students when admitted, and, in *all* others, that they found a congenial soil, when attempts were made to introduce them. Three young men, who were members of the Seminary about the period referred to, afterwards connected themselves with the Romanists.

When the history of the Seminary about this period, both as regards some of its internal elements and many of the outward agencies which were brought to bear upon it, is calmly and dispassionately examined, the conclusion must force itself on every thoughtful mind, that the difficulties may be traced to the natural influence of the Oxford Tracts. Apart from their generally deeper religious feeling, the principles which characterize these publications harmonize very much with those that distinguished the Jacobite party in the Church of England during the time of the Stuarts; although it may be that, in some respects, and as exhibited in a few of their productions, as, for instance, No. 90, the approximation to Roman Catholic error is closer. It is therefore not to be wondered at that men, whose views on disputed topics of discipline or doctrine were what are usually known as ultra High-Church, should have eagerly embraced them, and, in many cases, without any clear view of their nature and tendency. They were decidedly anti-sectarian, anti-Low-Church, and that was enough to enkindle the glow of affection. Such feeling, in a greater or less degree, influenced a considerable number of our clergy, and one or two members of the Faculty, who had always been known as High-Churchmen, participated in it. Several of the young men, too, who entered the Seminary, had imbibed the same spirit, and were ready to affirm statements of doctrine, of the meaning of which they had no clear idea. The phraseology and the supposed doctrines were thought to be Church-like, and the propriety and correctness of both were, perhaps unconsciously, assumed. The cant in common use among a certain class of persons was: "The Church says so, and that's enough." If asked, "What do you mean by the Church?—where has she said so?—how do you know that such is her meaning?"—the questions were regarded with suspicion, as if they implied setting up private judgment against the Church. Thus, as has always been the case in such controversy, the thing to be proved was taken for granted.

But although there certainly were students who ran into extremes on points of this sort, and were sustained in certain of their notions somewhat by officials within the Seminary, and in a much greater degree by clergymen without, yet such views did not, either at that period or any other, characterize the mass, and unqualified charges have often been advanced against the institution which were unfounded. The truth of this remark will appear to any impartial man who will examine the catalogues for a few years, trace the ministerial history of the respective members of the several classes, and become acquainted with their ecclesiastical, parochial, and religious standing. It is unfair, ungenerous, and indeed dishonorable, to select a few names noted for ultra views, extraordinary procedure, and want of practical success in the ministry, and exhibit them as a sample of Seminary training, ignoring at the same time their fellow-students, who have spent years of laborious, useful activity in building up the Church, it may be in retired places, where their daily efforts were unknown, except in the immediate vicinity of those who were blessed by their ministrations. On the one hand, the Seminary must not pretend to claim the merit of all the valuable labors of her best sons ; nor, on the other, is she chargeable with the weakness, inefficiency, erroneous or mistaken views, or conduct, of young men who entered her walls under the influence of a particular theological system, contemptuously rejected the instructions which might have served to clear, in some degree, the misty atmosphere of their minds, and passed out of the Institution radically unchanged. The real fault is farther back, and may be found in the right answer to to the all-important and suggestive question: "Who recommended these youths as apt and meet to exercise the ministry to the glory of God and the good of the Church?" Under the influence of what genial suns, of what gentle showers, of what balmy dews, did these saplings grow, so as to supply suitable materials for ministerial Mercuries?

On the twenty-eighth of June, 1848, Dr. Wilson sent to the Trustees a resignation of his professorship, which he withdrew the next day, at "the earnest and unanimous wish of the Board." In 1850, however, he renewed the act, and the resignation was accepted. So also was Dr. Moore's, which was tendered at the same time. The Trustees passed suitable resolutions in relation to both, and appointed them *emeriti* professors in their respective departments. The students gave evidence of regard for their venerated teachers by presenting to each a beautiful quarto Bible, also to the Seminary Chapel a very handsome silver chalice and paten for the communion, inscribed with their names. At a special meeting, held November fifth, 1850, Dr. Samuel R. Johnson was appointed successor to Dr. Wilson. The same year the Rev. Mr. Houghton was appointed instructor in Hebrew by the Standing Committee, who had been "requested to supply such instruction as may be needed in the elements of the language." (See Proceedings, November fifth and September twenty-fourth, pages 668 and 655.)

Early in 1851, Dr. Ogilby, whose health had long been failing, died in Paris. On the tenth of September the Rev. Milo Mahan, A.M., was appointed his successor.

CHAPTER X.

Serious Personal Injury—Record of Publications—"Essay on our Lord's Discourse at Capernaum"—"Biographical Notices of Jewish Rabbis"—Dr. Murdock's opinion of the Work—"Spiritual Things Compared with Spiritual"—Reply to Strictures upon the Publication—Two Discourses on the Rule of Faith— A Volume on Prophecy—The Epistle to the Hebrews in Greek and English—The Epistle to the Romans in Greek and English—The Epistle to the Ephesians in Greek and English—The Epistle to the Galatians in Greek and English.

EARLY in October, 1853, on crossing the North River in the Jersey City ferry-boat, I had a very violent fall, and injured my right thigh so severely that, for a day or two, the physician was doubtful whether some fracture had not taken place. Happily, this was not the case. For more than a month I could not move without great difficulty. After that time, however, I was able, with occasional omissions, to attend the classes in my study. Late in the winter I became strong enough to walk out a little by the aid of crutches, the use of which I could not abandon until the end of the next summer. From the effects of this fall I have never been entirely relieved.

The day after my accident, at the Triennial Meeting of the Trustees, held on the eleventh of the month, Bishop Potter of Pennsylvania proposed to raise the salaries of the Professors of Systematic Divinity and Ecclesiastical History to $2000 each, and "in consideration of long, laborious, and inadequately paid services," (see Proceedings, October, 1853, page 843,) to raise mine to $2500. Originally it was $1000, after the removal of the Seminary from New-Haven $1500, to which, on the erection of a building, a residence therein was added. The expenses of housekeeping, which for several years had been steadily advancing, made an addition to the salaries not only desirable, but necessary.

I now go back a few years to give an account of some publications which I had caused to be issued after that on Genesis.

During the summer of 1844, it was told me, by an intelligent and well-educated student from the Diocese of Maine, that, during a visit which he had lately made at West-Point, he was surprised to find some Episcopalians, who had been very favorably impressed by Dr. (afterwards Cardinal) Wiseman's Lectures on the Real Presence. I was thus led to examine the book, and finding that it abounded with unsound reasoning and interpretation, and contained some misstatements of facts, indicating extraordinary want of knowledge and attention, as to the particulars concerned, I undertook to show its inconsistencies and errors, and at the same time to prepare an analysis and exposition of our Lord's Discourse at Capernaum, which the Cardinal had misapprehended, and to present the reader with the views on this portion of St. John which had been given by the fathers of the first three centuries, and some of the earliest and leading divines of the Reformed Church of England. The result of this investigation was published in 1845, under the title: *Essay on our Lord's Discourse at Capernaum, recorded in the sixth chapter of St. John*, 12mo, pp. 158; to which in 1851 I added a short appendix.

As illustrative of the feeling which existed in some minds in reference to my theological views, and the kind of instruction known to be given by me in the Seminary, I will quote the language which was applied to this Essay, in a note appended to a sermon published by the Reverend gentleman, to whom the author of the *Record of Councils*, before mentioned, acknowledges himself indebted for information respecting the state of the Church in this country. (See page 201.) He represents the interpretation of John 6 as " a comparatively novel and neological exposition, put forth to supplant the teaching of the Catholic Church on the holy mystery of the body and blood of Christ."

In studying Jewish Commentaries, I had been in the habit of committing to paper translations of certain portions, especially such as seemed to be particularly important to Christian biblical students. After some time I undertook to translate entire, the exposition given by their most distinguished writers of some select portions of the prophets, especially of Isaiah, together with a few passages from the Targums. To these I added some selections from the *Jad and More Nevochim* of Maimonides. To all these I appended a few notes and appropriate introductions. Short biographical notices of the authors, whose works afforded the material for translation, preceded the selected portions. This volume was issued in 1847, under the following title: *Biographical Notices of some of the most Distinguished Jewish Rabbies, and Translations of Portions of their Commentaries and other Works, with illustrative Introductions and Notes.* Stanford & Swords. 12mo, 1847, pp. 245. While study-

10

ing these Rabbinical productions, I employed myself in preparing, from lexicographical authorities, a glossary of such words as either do not occur in the Hebrew Bible, or not with the later Jewish meaning. Connected with the Glossary was a large table of abbreviations, selected chiefly from the work of Buxtorf. In the preface to the *Notices*, etc., I pledged myself to publish the Glossary and Abbreviations, provided "this little volume should be fortunate enough to secure a patronage sufficient to meet the expense of its publication." I did hope to add also the original selections in Rabbinic. However, I have not yet, in fourteen years, been required to redeem the pledge; and subsequent various occupations have made me rather rusty in this sort of knowledge.

As I had formed a slight acquaintance with two or three Jewish gentlemen who were somewhat familiar with the original works of their own *literati*, I sent them copies of my book. From one, who occasionally acted as reader in a synagogue, I received a very courteous note in Hebrew. In the midst of no little Oriental laudation, he expressed his dissent from some of my statements. My answer, which was of course in English, reciprocated his courtesy, and offered to consider any objections which he might be pleased to communicate. Our correspondence, however, ended with my reply.

In the *Church Review* for April, 1848, there is a notice of this work, which contains the following: "To the correctness of the translations from Jarchi and some of the Targums, *we ourselves can testify.* The tract from the More Nevochim, or Guide to the Perplexed, *we have compared throughout with the original Hebrew,* and pronounce it accurate and scholar-like." I give this extract, because the remarks were written by the late venerable and Rev. James Murdock, D.D., than whom few men were more competent to give a correct opinion, and none more certain to give such as he believed to be true.

The next year I published a pamphlet of eighty pages, for the immediate use of theological students in their critical examination of the New Testament, intending it at the same time for Bible-classes, and private Christians who might be willing to take some trouble in order to ascertain the meaning of sacred Scripture. I gave it the title: *Spiritual Things. Compared with Spiritual, and Explained to Spiritual Men; or an Attempt to Illustrate the New Testament by Parallel References.* The

allusion which it contains, to a meaning of 1
Corinthians 2 : 13, different from that of our
authorized translation, is explained in the Preface, which states, also, the design of the publication. By putting it into the hands of Seminary students, I have been saved the trouble
of dictating, and they of copying a multiplici-
ty of references. I intended it as, in a measure,
a Biblical Comment on the New Testament.
On the appearance of this volume, which, although quite small, had given me a good deal
of trouble, it was noticed in a Church paper.
I thought it expedient to vindicate the References from its strictures, and therefore published two articles in the *Protestant Churchman*
of May twenty-seventh, and June tenth, 1848.
The editor of the former periodical " could not
imagine upon what ground all allusion to the
Holy Eucharist was avoided" in the references
on John 6 : 52–56. I stated, in reply, that, as I
had "taken some pains in the Essay" previously mentioned, "to show that the discourse recorded in the sixth chapter of St. John does
not *relate directly* to the Eucharist, and that
any part of it can only be *indirectly applied*
thereto with propriety, I purposely omitted
any reference to that institution, lest the reader
should think that I intended to teach a direct

relation of the one to the other." I referred, also, to the view of that Discourse, as given by "Whitby, Hammond, Waterland, Beveridge, and Cranmer, among the Church of England divines, with that of Erasmus, of the Church of Rome."

The reviewer's next remark was as follows: "Our authorized version, in the margin, parallels with verse 52, Matthew 26 : 26, 28. We suppose that the authority of our translators ought not lightly to be set aside." I replied to this in full : " Our authorized version has been repeatedly published with parallel references, varying in different editions. It is a mere assumption to say that the authority of any such collation is equal to that of the translation. The old editions, both of King James's Bible and of the translations that preceded it, contain very few references. It is the later editions which have multiplied them. If the question is tried by Tertullian's rule — id est verum quodcunque primum, id est adulterum quodcunque posterius—the remark about *lightly setting aside authority, and the parallels of our authorized version* must be retracted. Let us look at the FACTS.

" CRANMER's Bible, 1539, has very few references, and on John 6, *does not refer* to Matt.

26 : 26, 28. The BISHOP'S BIBLE, 1575, has very few, and none on John 6 : 52–67. The GENEVAN, printed by Robert Barker, in London, 1584, does not refer to the text in Matthew, but does to 1 Cor. 11 : 27, and so also Barker's New Testament of 1605. Beza's 'English edition by L. Tomson,' and printed by Barker in 1601, has no reference to Matt. 26. King James's Bible of 1611, contains very few references in general; on John 6, only fifteen, and none to Matt. 26." I proceeded to refer to many other early authorities from 1613 to 1671, and then asked what was meant by *"the parallels of our authorized version,* and the *setting aside of the authority of our translators?* If the charge of setting aside authority could be alleged at all, it would be against those who refer to Matt. 26, and those who advocate the reference. But I waive the advantage which the incautious remark has given me, as I do not admit the principle assumed. The references have not the same authority as the text. In all the editions the text is intended to be the same, not so the references. And to what edition are we to go for the authoritative ones?" *

* These remarks have a very direct bearing on the controversy respecting the standard Bible, which arose in connection with the action of the American Bible Society in 1857, and will be afterwards noted.

The next remark in the notice is this: "To say nothing of Catholic antiquity." The inclination to censure on the same ground as that which was taken against certain portions of the *Companion to Genesis*, appears in this short clause. I set it aside with that plainness which I thought the attempt deserved. "It is not at all uncommon to assume a consent of fathers in behalf of some favorite exposition, whereon some equally favorite dogma is thought to be sustained, and then to ring the changes of the favorite strain of an ideal catholicity. The term catholic, and its cognate expressions, have become with certain persons vague and indefinite epithets. We hear of catholic architecture, catholic poetry, catholic music, catholic usages, most of which were confined to very limited localities, and originated in comparatively late periods. I have no thought of denying a real catholicity on leading points. A catholicity in the great and fundamental doctrines of the Gospel, and in the facts and institutions which serve to develop and prove them, I not only admit, but delight to recognize and avow. But I must say, that the view of John 6 : 53–56, which explains it of the Eucharist, is not supported by Catholic antiquity. To prove such authority an induction of many particulars is necessary. Quotations must be adduced and examined. A concurrent series of writers must be produced. An isolated allusion or clause, in one or two fathers, proves nothing. The careful inquirer will ask, what is the evidence afforded by an examination of the whole? and this implies an accurate comparison of each with the other." The third part of the Essay on John 6, is then referred to for " the most important passages in Catholic antiquity, as they are there given in the original Greek and Latin, and translated into English," on passages in that chapter, " which *some moderns* have understood as directly intended of the Eucharist." I went somewhat at large into that " interpretation of our Lord's discourse which makes it relate directly to the Eucharist," which I designated as a *"private, not Catholic"* exposition, and gave an account of the discussion which took place on this point at the Council of Trent, showing, from Pallavicini, that that body did not venture to appeal to Catholic interpretation of this discourse in reference to the Lord's Supper. This part of the communication I afterwards incorporated in an Appendix to a second edition of the Essay, which was published in 1851. Knowing how deeply and extensively rooted was the erroneous application of this discourse, and the unfounded supposition of its patristical explanation being sacramental, I availed myself of the occasion afforded to show the contrary. This I did at length, and with sufficiently full references.

In the next paper the reviewer repeated the old assertions, and referred to ancient writers by name. I had accommodated to his unproved statements and intimations the words of Juvenal—"*stat pro ratione*"—DICTUM. To this he replies thus: "He must be a queer man, indeed, to pass off his *dictum* instead of reason and argument, when the latter, in the shape of testimonies from Ignatius, Irenæus, Tertullian, Clemens Alexandrinus, Augustine, etc., etc., can be, as Professor Turner is well aware, so very cheaply obtained by any one who is ambitious to make a display of quotations." Few readers of this sentence could suppose that what the writer represents as not only susceptible of proof, but familiar to all well-read theologians, is entirely unfounded, and without even a shadow of evidence. This I stated in the plainest terms. "I assure the writer that I was not aware that these testimonies could be obtained so cheaply. Indeed I know they can not be obtained at any price. The reader will

10*

bear in mind that the point at issue is the eucharistic or sacramental interpretation of John 6, assumed to be given by those writers, not what they may say about the Eucharist. If the reviewer can so easily get reason and argument in the shape of testimonies to this effect from these Fathers, let him produce them, and thus entitle himself to the merit of the discovery. This is the very thing I have called on him to do, and which I know he can not do; and for this plain reason, *that they are not to be found in these writers.* I must therefore say again, that instead of proof we have assertion." Here the controversy ended.

On the third Sunday in Advent, December sixteenth, 1849, it became my turn to address the students on occasion of the matriculation of the Junior class. I selected a subject which was appropriate in general to my department of Interpretation, and also particularly adapted to meet certain vague and undefined notions, of which what has just been quoted affords a specimen. I called attention to the sacred Scriptures as the sole rule of faith, founding my two discourses on the words of the Psalmist, "The entrance of thy word giveth light," (119 : 130.) One or two portions are selected to show the nature of the principle maintained and the plainness with which I brought it out.

"We return then to the query suggested by the affirmation of the text—where shall we find this word of God, the entrance of which giveth light? A reply, sufficiently laconic, was once almost universally given to this question, namely, in the Church; and it has been repeated with and without exposition and limitation—ask the Church. If this direction be intended to imply that the Church is properly the fountain of Divine light, it is untrue, and contradicted by unequivocal statements in our own standards of faith, by frequent declarations of the earliest and best of the fathers. In this sense, the general direction to draw the truth from the Church, as its fountain, involves many particulars, each of which must be clearly settled before we can ever be prepared to apply it. What is the Church? Who compose it? What constitutes membership? What is necessary for legitimate initiation? Does the direction relate to the Church now? or in certain past ages? or in all its phases of existence? As the alleged source of religious light, has the Church always been invariably the same? and if so, has she the essential property of never teaching error? On what ground is such infallibility predicated? If of Scripture, where are the texts, and who is to expound them? If of reason, where is there even a show of evidence? and who is to judge of it? How is the assumption to be reconciled with the demonstrable fact, that certain doctrines of one age have been maintained in contradiction to those of another — both classes being equally authoritative? Does the Church speak through the whole mass of her members? or through a majority? or through the faithful only? and if so, who is to discriminate these among the visible mass, and to select the wheat from among the tares? or is it through some one claiming to be universal head? and who or what is he? and where are his credentials? Or again, is it through her ecclesiastical officers? And are all of them the medium, or only a moiety? If the latter, of what grade? Or, if so groundless a claim be rejected, and it be admitted that, at various times and places, the instructions of the Church have varied, how are we to know when and where she has been right? If her teaching should be thought to be equivocal or doubtful, who has the right and ability to interpret the interpreter? It is not to be expected that

vague or unproved statements on these and
other kindred theological topics will be blind-
ly admitted by men of intelligence. They do
but perpetuate controversy without eliciting
truth. The Church, by which I mean the
body of Christians that have lived, and do
live, and shall continue to live on the earth,
proclaiming the living word, and rightly administering and receiving the divinely instituted sacraments, is no infallible source of the
truth. It is indeed its 'pillar and ground,' its
firmly established support. It is its 'keeper
and witness,' the consecrated ark overshadowed
by the cherubim, preserving those tables of the
divine law which 'were written by the finger
of God.' This character of the Church sets her
up as 'the standard for the nations,' and makes
her publicly call them to flock to the banner
of that mighty conqueror, whose 'rest shall be
glorious.' It kindles, on the shore of the
ever-troubled sea of mistiness and doubt, that
lofty beacon-light, which, supplied with the
holy oil of the sanctuary, shall never go out,
but burn and flame and blaze in a celestial
splendor, until its divine warmth and illumination shall have dissipated error, and shall
have animated and attracted to itself all the
tempest-tossed and perishing. But the Church

can only preserve, can only show forth, illustrate, impress divine truth. She can not originate one particle of that holy light, which owes its being to the Father of illumination, of whom alone it is the first-born offspring."

As I could not comprise all that I wished to incorporate in the matriculation address within the limits of one discourse, on the afternoon of the same day I resumed the subject, examining the inquiry how God's word may enter into the heart and understanding so as to give light. I laid down three leading directions, resolving them into the duty of prayer and dependence on the Author of divine illumination, the exercise of sound sense and good judgment, and the acquisition of a competent acquaintance with holy Scripture in the original. These points I endeavored to develop and impress. The discourses were published at the request of the students, with notes appended. They are entitled: *Light in the Church, God's Word, the Source of Divine Light, and how it may be most successfully studied.* I have reason to think that its open development of important Protestant truth, was not without its use. Though it exposed, both in the discourses and notes, some favorite representations of not a few, no attempt was made to overthrow its statements or reasonings.

During the spring and summer of 1851, I delivered in the Seminary Chapel seven discourses on Prophecy. The subjects treated of were, its divine origin, its increasing development and certainty, the various ways in which it was communicated, prophetic vision, prophetic simile and figure, and the qualifications of the interpreter. To these I added another on the blessing of Japhet, though it did not make a part of the series. These eight discourses I published at the request of the students, accompanying them with suitable notes. They make a 12mo volume of 219 pages.

In attending to the duties of my department I had found by experience that but few young men obtained any clear insight into the meaning of difficult texts by a mere reference to various commentators. Such a course frequently produced confusion of mind, and moreover required more time than the Seminary arrangements allowed. It had therefore been my invariable practice for many years to lecture on all the portions of Scripture which I intended to make the subject of recitation. The materials for these lectures were written in an in-

terleaved New Testament, the London edition
of Griesbach of 1818. I had frequently been
requested by some of the more studious and
intelligent members of the Seminary to publish a Greek Testament with notes, so condensed as not to exceed two volumes. I knew
that this would not admit of such an exegesis
as a careful examination of many portions
would demand, in order to satisfy an intelligent and conscientious inquirer, and that the
enterprise would result in a meagre and unsatisfactory production. I therefore determined to
select some of the most important portions of
the New Testament, and to prepare an exposition of them, without being limited in space,
but guided by the nature of the subjects involved. I began with the Epistle to the Hebrews, selecting this book, because the notes
which I had already accumulated on it were
considerable, and also because an exegetical investigation of its various portions appeared to
be particularly appropriate in the state of the
Church at that time. I had been, for years, in
the habit of directing the attention of the
classes to the subject of quotations in the New
Testament from the Old, not so much with
reference to their verbal conformity either to
the original Hebrew or the Septuagint Trans-

lation, as to that of the thought and general purport. The notes on this point, which I had prepared for lecturing on the second chapter of St. Matthew, I incorporated with the Comment on Hebrews 1 : 5, because of their adaptation to this and other passages in the chapter. Had I begun with the Gospels, I should have much preferred introducing this matter in connection with the early part of St. Matthew. The volume was published in 1852, with the title, *The Epistle to the Hebrews, in Greek and English, with an Analysis and Exegetical Commentary.* I afterwards added an Appendix, containing a series of questions on the entire book. The whole volume amounted to 200 pages 8vo.

The next year I published a similar volume of 252 pages on the Romans, with the Greek type much improved. I dedicated this volume to the memory of Bishop White, to whom, when living, I had addressed my first production on the same Epistle in 1824. The publisher threw the dedication into the form of an urn.

Early in the spring of 1856, I published a third volume of Commentary, namely, on the Ephesians, pages 198. This I dedicated to my friend, the Rev. Christian Frederic Crusé, D.D.

In the autumn of the same year I added a small volume of 98 pages on the Galatians. My original intention was to unite these two in one volume; but, after both were prepared for the press, I saw an announcement of Jowett's work on the latter Epistle, and deferred printing my own until I should have examined it. My present intention is to unite the Romans and Galatians in one volume, on account of the connection of the main subject of each Epistle.

CHAPTER XI.

Plain-Song in the Seminary—Mr. Hopkins—Pastoral Care of the Students—The American Bible Society—His Relation to it—The Standard Bible—The Fortieth Anniversary of his Professorship—Sketch of Dr. Wilson—General Review.

I SHALL now proceed, briefly, to state three particulars, two of which bear on my connection with the Seminary, and the other on that with the American Bible Society.

At a meeting of the Trustees, held on June twenty-eighth, 1855, the following resolution was passed:

"*Resolved*, That the Standing Committee be, and is hereby empowered, to provide for the students of the Seminary, instruction in vocal sacred music." [*]

Under this resolution of the Board, the Rev. John Henry Hopkins, Jr., was appointed instructor by the Standing Committee, and this was sanctioned by the Trustees at a subsequent meeting.[†] Mr. Hopkins entered on the duties of his office in November, and made a report

[*] See Proceedings, etc., June twenty-eighth, 1855, page 40.

[†] See the Proceedings at the Triennial Meeting, September twenty-ninth, 1856, page 114.

in June, 1856. The following year, June twenty-third, a second very brief report was submitted, and some time afterwards the instructor resigned.

In the early part of 1856 a difference of opinion arose in reference to the Chapel music. The lately appointed teacher, at the request, as I was informed, of a majority of the students, accepted the place of organist. In this capacity, and also in that of instructor, he introduced the kind of chanting which is known by the name of "plain song," to the exclusion, in a great degree, of the music before in use. A very large proportion of the students was opposed to this novelty. One of the consequences was, that the number who attended his instructions became much reduced, and not a few were unwilling to take part in a service so characterized. Ever since the regular morning and evening services of the Church had been used, in accordance with the direction of the Trustees, the mode of celebrating them had, in all particulars, been under the control of the officiating professor; and, as the students had generally made such arrangements as were in nowise objectionable, and frequently highly commendable in point of musical taste and religious feeling, the officiating professors scarcely ever had any occasion to interfere with their arrangements. Thus things went on harmoniously. The chanting of the Psalter, (introduced by Dr. Ogilby,) I had always objected to, inasmuch as it was against the ordinary usage of our Church; and, in my opinion, neither rubrical nor in character with the Institution, as a General Seminary, intended for the whole Church. In this particular I stood alone, not objecting, however, to the arrangements of my brother professors, who, on their part, never objected to mine.

On the introduction of the plain-song chanting by the Reverend Instructor who had taken the place of organist, I addressed a note to him, claiming the right, as officiating professor, to control the music when it was my turn to read the service, and requesting, on such occasions, the omission of that style of chanting. To my great surprise, the musical instructor and organist claimed this right himself, *ex officio*, and declined acceding to my views. To his communications I made one reply, which I supposed would be satisfactory and agreeable. His answer confirmed my previously formed determination, and I refused to yield, in any degree, what I regarded both as my official right and duty. Mr. Hopkins therefore refused to act as organist on the days when I read the service. Consequently, some anti-plain-song student presided at the organ on such occasions. This was quite gratifying to me, as I never thought "plain-song" either agreeable to a musical ear, or devotional in its impression.

At a meeting of the Trustees, held in Trinity Church, October sixteenth, 1832, the office of Dean of the Faculty was instituted, each of the resident professors being directed to exercise its rights and attend to its duties annually in succession.* The first report was made by me June twenty-fifth, 1833; the second by Dr. Wilson June twenty-fifth, 1834; and the next, as recorded in the Proceedings of the Trustees, by Professor Whittingham, June twenty-fourth, 1837.† Notice of this appointment appears also in the statutes published in 1836.‡ The following amendment was passed in 1837:

"He shall, also, during the term of his office, be charged with the public religious instruction and the pastoral care of the students."§

Next year the office devolved on me; and in the report which, as Dean, I made to the Trus-

---

* See Proceedings, ubi sup. page 367.

† Ubi sup. pages 413, 462, 585, 586.

‡ See chapter vi. section 2, pages 16, 17.

§ Proceedings, pages 619, 626.

tees, I submitted to their consideration the following remarks:

The undersigned "has always regarded the pastoral care, even of an ordinary congregation, as comprising duties of great interest and importance, not to be undertaken without careful examination and conscientious conviction of duty. The pastoral care of a number of theological students preparing for the ministry, he could not but consider as a charge still more solemn in its character, involving a responsibility, than which scarcely any can be greater, and not to be imposed without the consent of the person sustaining the office of pastor. Still, it was the desire of the Dean to meet the wishes of the Trustees as far as he consistently could, by giving to the students 'the public religious instruction' which the statute enjoins. It was at first his intention to meet the students in the Seminary Chapel on Sunday mornings for public worship and sermon. Such services had been performed there by Professor Wilson and himself during several years, before the Chapel of St. Peter's was built. But a practical difficulty immediately suggested itself. Soon after entering the Seminary, almost all the students became connected with different churches in the city, both as members under the rectors, who exercise towards them the same pastoral relation which they exercise towards the other members of their congregations, and also as superintendents or teachers in the respective Sunday-schools belonging to the congregations of which they constitute a part. Was it expedient for the Dean to require an attendance which would destroy this connection? Was it the intention of the Trustees that he should do this, and call away the students from duties useful to themselves and beneficial to others, and in which young men preparing for the ministry ought chiefly to be interested? A third service, after the fatigue of Sunday-school instruction during the day, appeared to him to be, in general, neither agreeable nor useful. Embarrassed by these considerations, and unable to discover by private conversation with individual Trustees, that they had been in contemplation when the resolution was passed, he has not given 'public religious instruction,' neither has he considered himself as sustaining 'a pastoral relation' to the students."* The report of Dr. Haight, also a Dean, made June twenty-fifth, 1850, incorporated an account of my action as " chaplain" during the

* Proceedings, ubi sup. pages 640, 641.

preceding year, with a renewal of this statement, that I "could not consent, for reasons satisfactory to myself, to undertake the pastoral care of the students."

In my report of June, 1855, I brought this point again before the Board, and insert therefrom the following extracts:

"With that part of the requisition before referred to, which intrusts 'the whole pastoral care of the students' to the Dean, it becomes my duty to say that I have not complied. It is not my purpose, as it certainly would not be within my province, to enter at all into the question of the expediency (according to the usual analogy of the ecclesiastical regulations and action in our Church) of requiring a communicant to change his pastoral relations on becoming a member of the Seminary, or a professor to assume the obligations of a proper pastoral charge. It is certainly optional with the one to decline to enter the Seminary, and with the other to accept a professorship on such a condition. But the obligation of undertaking such condition, when superadded to the original terms, is quite a different consideration. The chief reason of my unwillingness to be regarded as the students' pastor, I will state with that frankness which ought to characterize

11

every right-minded man, and which a long connection with the Seminary may the rather justify me in employing. The ordinary pastoral
duties, those, namely, of religious service and
instruction, of attention and consolation, also, in
occasional sickness, I am quite willing in my
turn to perform. But there is another duty
incumbent on a pastor, which, if fully exercised
in all cases, might bring a Dean into collision
with some rectors, and, it may be, Standing
Committees and Bishops. The pastor is expected to recommend the candidate for Holy
Orders as 'worthy to be admitted thereto.'
(Canon XV. of 1832.) I can not pledge myself
to do this for every student whose testimonial
of having properly attended to the prescribed
course of study I may be fully authorized to
sign. On the contrary, it may happen that, as
pastor, I should sometimes be obliged to dis-
courage a student from taking upon him the
ministerial office. This would not necessarily imply deficiency in his moral or religious
character. It might be founded on an apparent
want of other essential qualifications. And I
do not hesitate to say that I am not stating a
hypothetical case. But here a professor might
readily fall into a mistake, as he can not be
supposed to know a young man so thoroughly

as the 'minister of the parish,' who, for a course of years, has had him under his own inspection and spiritual training. Still, the Seminary pastor must act on his own conviction of duty; and this, as was before remarked, might bring him into unpleasant conflict of opinion with some of his brethren. In stating this difficulty, I have gone on the supposition that, by the phrase, 'the *whole* pastoral care of the students,' in the statute before referred to, the intention was to constitute the Dean *their sole pastor*, a meaning which seems to be the only legitimate one.

"On the other hand, I not only grant, but am deeply impressed by the conviction, that for those students who have not been brought up in this city, and who consequently can enjoy no accustomed pastoral supervision during their Seminary course, it is all-important to provide, in connection with the Institution, a truly pastoral head, who shall feel the duty and obligation, and have also the right, untrammelled by any other pastoral authority, to train those committed to his charge, and, as his observation and knowledge may dictate, to encourage them or not in their preparation for the ministry. But I submit whether an annual change of the Pastor is likely to produce any efficient practical result."*

The above remarks are here introduced in corroboration of the opinion before expressed. No communication has ever been made by the Trustees to the Faculty on this subject, or interview held with them by any Committee appointed for such purpose. The Statute remains unaltered.† Whether the appointment of Dean as "Chaplain, intrusted with the whole pastoral care of the students," destroys all rights and obligations of a city Rector of whose congregation a student may have been a member from infancy; or whether the Statute regards him as under the supervision of two pastors, who may or may not agree in recommending him for the ministry; also, what influence an official position is likely to have which is to be relinquished at the expiration of one year, then occupied by another professor, and at some future time reässumed by the former, it is not my intention to note. I will only add that, in accordance with the resolution of Dr. Wilson and myself, not to accede to the Statute, I have always declined to sign the testi-

---

* Proceedings, June twenty-seventh, twenty-eighth, 1855, pp. 14, 15.

† See Constitution and Statutes, published October, 1860, Chapter 6, Section 2, page 26.

monials of students for admission into the Ministry, referring them to their respective Rectors; and also, in the cases of strangers, who always constitute a large majority, to those city pastors with whose congregations they became connected.

The other matter before alluded to is so generally and extensively known, that I shall restrict myself to a very few remarks, some of which are rather of a private nature.

The *Church Review*, (a quarterly publication, issued at New-Haven,) of October, 1856, Volume IX., No. 3, page 422, contained some strictures on the Standard Bible, which the Managers of the American Bible Society had lately issued with more than usual laudation. The Committee on Versions, of which I was a member, to whose care its preparation had some years before been intrusted, had introduced some slight alterations in the spelling, particularly of two or three proper names, occasionally also as to capital letters, punctuation, and frequently in the headings at the tops of pages and over chapters. In the translation itself no change had been made, except the introduction of the definite article in connection with the name of John. A portion of those strictures seemed to me to have an unjust bearing on the conduct of the Managers, and particularly on that of the Committee on Versions. I therefore replied to it in the next number, pages 547–560. The subject of the alterations introduced in the Standard Bible soon became prominent in the ecclesiastical or religious papers of various denominations. Some misapprehensions, and also some misrepresentations, were published. In many English and some American editions of King James's Bible, matter had been introduced at various times for two centuries, by individuals, and independently of any civil or ecclesiastical authority. The most prominent of these publications, together with the original edition of the authorized translation, which made its appearance in 1611, had been very carefully examined by the Committee. The members who were most prominent in carrying out this laborious undertaking were, Dr. Robinson, Professor in the Union Theological Seminary, and Dr. Vermilye. Occasionally I attended the meetings, and I think the Rev. Dr. Storrs also. The Rev. Dr. McLane had been appointed to examine certain leading editions, and to state the various differences, in order the better to prepare us for deciding on the particulars to be reported for action on the part of the Committee, at their numerous meetings. In this position he labored with most extraordinary industry and care, and presented the results of his efforts, with conscientious fidelity to his trust, in thousands of various readings and methods accurately written out. Thus some of the various accessions, which in course of time had been appended to the published version, and some also of those which had been added by the translators themselves, were somewhat modified, radically altered, or entirely removed; and, I may well say, that in many cases a marked improvement was made, by the unanimous consent of the Committee on Versions. But this was often represented as a change of the version itself, which had been left unaltered.

As some publications by the author of the original article in the *Church Review,* and particularly by certain prominent Presbyterian members of the Society, made their appearance, and became the more disseminated and known, the excitement increased very greatly. Not a few of the leading Managers took the ground, that the Constitution so connected the generally prevailing punctuation, parentheses, spelling, capitals, headings, and references, which were in common use when the Society was formed, with the text itself, as to compre-

hend both under the name of the Authorized
English Version. Hence they inferred that the
Society could not rightly give its sanction to
any change in these particulars. Thus they
avowed their purpose never to allow any thing
to be admitted into their editions which had
not been published half a century before, and
to stereotype *in perpetuum* headings and other
accessory matters which tended naturally to
perpetuate some erroneous notions in the mind
of the ordinary reader. Almost all the members of the Committee on Versions maintained
the opposite principle, namely, that the Constitution simply prohibited any change of *the
text.* Yet even this involved an examination
of the question,—What, in no small number of
places where the texts, of various old editions
differed from each other, was the true original
reading? The object which the very distinguished and judicious founders of the Society
had in view was to perpetuate and extend the
revealed Word of God, known by the name of
THE BIBLE, and particularly what was known
as the authorized English VERSION of King
James.

The discussions which arose at various full
meetings of the Managers, the resolution which
was passed to require the Committee to carry

into effect the principle before stated, and thereby to prepare another standard edition to supersede the former, and their refusal to permit a protest against certain resolutions passed at one of the meetings, (which protest was signed by six of the whole eight members of the Committee,) to be entered on the minutes of the meeting, led those members to resign their places. I was afterwards requested to accept a position in the new Committee about to be formed; but as I had resigned simply because I could not conscientiously acquiesce in the action of the Managers, nor adopt the principle which their resolutions enjoined, I declined the offer.

The numerous particulars connected with this complicated topic which, as the controversy advanced, became the more developed, tended to show that the history of our highly venerated, and in very many respects most invaluable English Bible, was comparatively but little known. Many of the most prominent writers who expressed their opinion against the action of the Committee on Versions in preparing the afterwards rejected standard edition—splendidly bound folio copies of which had been sent by the Managers, accompanied by the highest eulogies, to most of the crowned heads

11*

of Europe—were, in fact, wholly uninformed on the subject. Some took for granted that the version of 1611, in the exact form and position of the words, with the original appendages, had been handed down through successive generations, unaltered for nearly two hundred and fifty years. In order to set the truth of this matter in a clear light, I prepared a private letter, which I sent to a Right Rev. friend, whom I had known and highly esteemed for more than forty years, who had published a short article in one of our Church papers. I did not choose to enter into any public controversy on the much disputed, though little understood point, but availed myself of the opportunity to point out the generally prevailing mistakes, and to develop the truth by an induction in detail of incontrovertible statements.

Respecting the changes which had been made, and especially those in the headings, I publicly avowed to the Board of Managers that I would not undertake to defend the whole. Every member of such a committee could not be expected to have examined individually each one. I did not at all hesitate to acknowledge that many alterations might properly, and indeed ought to be made. And I have no doubt that if the whole matter had been again intrusted to the same Committee, with directions to reëxamine and improve the standard edition, the result would have given much more general, though not universal, satisfaction than will be the consequence of acting on the principle laid down by the Board. In that case I would have devoted myself to so important a work without passing over a single point unexamined. In the hope that some improvement with regard to headings might be introduced, I drew up a good many alterations, suggesting what appeared to me more appropriate than any in ordinary use. Those of Isaiah I revised with great care. In examining the Oxford quarto edition of 1852, I found several places at variance with the edition of 1611, and a comparison with those of the rejected standard evidently showed the great superiority of the latter in many respects, a good many of the others being not only unsupported by the text, but inconsistent with its plain meaning. But these manuscripts I set aside. Nevertheless, as the principle of providential action is *progress*, the time will come, sooner or later, when this whole matter must be revised and improved.

On June twenty-third, 1858, I addressed a

note to the Alumni of the Seminary, stating the time of my "appointment to a professorship," and inviting them to be present on the occasion of the fortieth anniversary of that appointment, when it was my intention to deliver an Address in St. Peter's Church. I received a very kind and affectionate reply, signed by their recording Secretary, the Rev. Morgan Dix, accepting the invitation.

On the night of the eighth of October, after the usual evening service and the delivery of the anniversary address,* I had the happiness of meeting many of my Rev. brethren, some of them my old pupils between thirty and forty years before, now well known as useful pastors, and several maintaining distinguished positions in the Church. Of the Bishops who had been students in the Seminary, the Right Rev. Drs. Whitehouse and Horatio Potter were present. The gratification was very greatly increased by an incident, to me entirely unexpected. Just before partaking of the evening collation, Bishop Whitehouse, who had graduated in 1824, addressed me in behalf of the Alumni, presenting me with a

---

* Three thousand copies of the Address were afterwards printed by the direction of the Alumni, and one thousand put into my hands for distribution, chiefly to future students.

paper commemorative of the fortieth anniversary of my appointment as professor, and kindly expressive of their regard. It was signed by a large number then present, and afterwards by several others, who were then living at a distance from the city. The paper was beautifully drawn up by the Rev. John Henry Hopkins, Jr., and ornamented with six drawings, illustrative of Scriptural facts bearing upon the period of forty days or years. From more than fifty pupils, living in various States, and some quite remote, I received very friendly letters, which, among others, some of earlier and some of later date, I hope to retain in possession until the end of life. I could not but feel that the complimentary remarks of the Right Rev. graduate of thirty-six years' standing were beyond my desert, and it was not without difficulty that I could command my feelings so as to make a suitable reply. The document presented by the Alumni I have preserved with great care, and shall ever regard this occasion as among the most interesting of my life.

About six months after the event just recorded, another occurred of a very different kind. My old friend and brother, the Rev. Dr. Wilson, whose health had been for a considerable time gradually declining, departed this life on the fourteenth of April, 1859, in his eighty-third year. The funeral services were performed in St. Peter's Church, of which he had been a constant attendant ever since its origin. His interment took place in the burial-ground of Christ Church, in Philadelphia, at the corner of Arch and Fifth streets, in the presence of a large body of the most respectable clergy and laymen. At the request of his niece, whom I had known from her childhood, in which also the clergy had united, at a meeting held immediately after the service at St. Peter's, I delivered there, on the eighth of May, a sermon in commemoration of the life and character of the deceased. It was published at the joint request of the clergy of New-York, and of the Faculty and Trustees of the Seminary. After some remarks on the doctrine of the resurrection, a topic which was adapted to the occasion, and particularly in accordance with the ecclesiastical time of the year, I gave a short sketch of Dr. Wilson's life and character. As this very able and excellent man, formerly a lawyer and judge, and afterwards a divine, always remarkable for retired habits and true Christian humility, was probably not much known in New-

York, I shall here introduce a page or two of the discourse, with references in support of the statements therein made.

"It is not my purpose to go into detail, but merely to state some prominent facts.*

"The Rev. Bird Wilson was the son of a gentleman of Scotland, who was born in 1742. The Hon. James Wilson was educated at Glasgow, St. Andrew's, and Edinburgh, and in part

* "The brief notice of Dr. Wilson's father was obtained chiefly from the following publications: 'Encyclopedia Americana,' Article—JAMES WILSON.—'Alexander Graydon's Memoirs of his Own Time,' edited by John Stockton Littell. 8vo. Phila.: Lindsay and Blakiston, 1846.—'History of the Origin, Formation, and Adoption of the Constitution of the United States,' by George Ticknor Curtis. 8vo, 2 vols. Harper and Brothers, N.Y., 1854. In this work, Judge Wilson is very favorably mentioned. The following extracts will show how highly he was appreciated: 'The life of this wise, able, and excellent man, was comparatively short. The character of his mind, and the sources of his influence, will be best appreciated by examining some of the more striking passages of his great speech on the Constitution.' This is followed by a note, covering fourteen closely printed pages, all of which is quoted from the speech referred to; vol. i. page 462, et seq. In vol. ii. page 520, he is represented as 'one of the wisest and ablest of the framers of the Constitution.

"For the few biographical statements respecting his son, I am indebted chiefly to private information, obtained from the most reliable sources. For the reader's satisfaction, I will mention the names of the Hon. Horace Binney, and the Rev. Jehu C. Clay, D.D., who for a time was rector of the Church at Norristown while Dr. Wilson was one of its wardens, and also that of Miss Hollingsworth, the Doctor's niece, who resided with him the greater part of the time that he lived in New-York. The kindness of these gentlemen and this most estimable lady in replying to my request for information, is hereby respectfully acknowledged.

under the supervision of Drs. Blair and Robertson, men universally celebrated for superior talent and learning. Soon after his arrival at Philadelphia, in the year 1766, he became a tutor in the College, and acquired a high reputation as a classical scholar. Entering on legal practice, first at Reading, and afterward at Carlisle, his abilities and acquisitions soon made him conspicuous. In 1775 he was elected a member of Congress. Being a uniform advocate of American independence, he signed the well-known Declaration. In 1787 he was a member of the Convention which framed the Constitution of the United States, and one of the Committee that reported the draft. Two years after he was appointed by Washington a Judge of the Supreme Court. He died at the age of fifty-six, leaving behind him three volumes of political and legal disquisitions, highly valued by intelligent men.

"The son inherited his father's talent, and in due time made himself equally conspicuous. Born January eighth, 1777, he graduated at the University of Pennsylvania, then known by the name of College, at the early age of fifteen, in the year 1792, about the time that the Rev. Dr. Ewing became Provost. He pursued the study of law, under the direction of

Joseph Thomas, of Philadelphia, aided, no doubt, by the abilities of his father. His early companions and friends were gentlemen who afterward attained a grade of eminence in their profession which few jurists in this country have ever reached.* Of Mr. Wilson it is not too much to say, accommodating the words of the Apostle, that he was 'not a whit behind the very chief of' his associates. In the exercise of his profession he was remarkable for the soundness of his counsels, founded on extensive knowledge of general principles and careful attention to the particular cases under consideration. He soon obtained a place in the office of the Commissioner of Bankrupt Law, and when a young man of only twenty-five, was appointed 'President Judge' of the Court of Common Pleas, in a judicial district composed of several of the eastern counties of Pennsylvania, and known as the Seventh Circuit. His residence was then at Norristown, where he was held in high respect and esteem for his virtues as a Christian man, and his integrity, uprightness and ability, as presiding officer of the Judiciary Department. In this hon-

---

* "Among the distinguished persons alluded to, it is sufficient to mention the names of Mr. Horace Binney, Messrs. Chauncey, and Mr. John Sergeant.

orable position it was his habit thoroughly to examine all accessible data bearing on any litigated matter in question. Keeping in mind all the points of evidence, great and small, on both sides, he weighed them in the balance of equity with the utmost scrupulousness, drew his conclusions with most logical accuracy, and formed his judgment with the most conscientious carefulness. Indeed Judge Wilson was so distinguished for the soundness of his decisions, that only one was ever reversed in a superior court, and that simply because he had not access to a document which contained such information on the case as, if known, would have modified his view.

"In the year 1813 the President Judge published Matthew Bacon's Abridgment of the Law, an English work, with considerable additions by a Barrister.* The American editor informs his readers that his object was 'to incorporate into' his publication 'the substance of the English decisions' which had been pass-

---

* "The title of this publication is as follows: A New Abridgment of the Law. By Matthew Bacon, of the Middle Temple, Esq. With considerable additions, by Henry Gwillim, of the Middle Temple, Esq., Barrister at Law. The first American, from the sixth London Edition; with the addition of the later English and the American Decisions. By Bird Wilson, Esq., President of the Court of Common Pleas in the Seventh Circuit of Pennsylvania. In seven volumes. Philadelphia. Published by Philip H. Nicklin. 1813.

ed since the appearance of the last London edition, 'together with the cases upon the same
subjects decided in America.' The preparation
of this work, which is in seven volumes, large
octavo, demanded great labor and research; and
the additions are characterized by the editor's
extensive investigations and well known accuracy.

"During the time that Judge Wilson resided at Norristown, he so employed his moral
and religious energies, as to induce the few
Episcopalians of the place to erect the church
which stands there at the present day. Of this
church he was warden for several years, and
a delegate to the Conventions of the diocese.

"His deeply religious character led him, on
an official occasion, when his kindly feelings
were more than usually wrought upon, to turn
his attention very decidedly to the sacred office
of the ministry, and on the twelfth of March,
1819, he was ordained Deacon, by the Right
Rev. Bishop White, in Christ Church, Philadelphia, and Priest about a year afterwards."
In a few years, the lately ordained Judge became a Professor in the General Seminary,
where he continued to give instruction in Systematic Divinity until June twenty-fifth, 1850.

Since the year 1853 I had been accustomed

to send certain articles to the *Parish Visitor*, in compliance with the request of the Editor. They consisted chiefly of expositions of some of our Lord's instructions, selected from the first three Gospels. Thinking that, if collected together, and somewhat improved by a few alterations and additions, a volume might be constructed, which would be useful to thoughtful readers of the New Testament, and particularly to all Sunday-school teachers, and also to the more religious and intelligent of their pupils, I published, towards the close of the year 1859, a volume of two hundred and fifty-eight pages, entitled, *Teachings of the Master, with an attempt to explain and enforce them. By a Disciple.* It contains twenty-five Essays, beginning with John's announcement of the Kingdom of Heaven, and ending with his Lord's reply to the Sadducees in defense of the doctrine of the resurrection. The wood-cut which precedes the title-page was copied from a very beautiful picture, which some of Dr. Muhlenberg's affectionate pupils had presented to him, as a memorial of their esteem and high appreciation of his worth. The celebrated Hübner, by whom it had been painted, was informed by the Rev. owner, that he regarded it as the most lovely and perfect symbol of

Protestantism that he had ever seen. The gifted artist expressed his great gratification by replying that, to produce a proper symbol of that religious system which regards the sacred Scriptures as the sole rule of faith, was the very motive by which he had been governed.

In the hope that this volume might be made useful, in accordance with its author's intentions, I had it in contemplation to publish a second, on selections from St. John's Gospel. I therefore prepared two Essays, explanatory of the Saviour's address to Nathanael, in 1 : 48–51, and of his statement to the unbelieving Jews, in 2 : 19, with the accompanying remarks. These were introduced in the same monthly periodical. After devoting a good deal of time and attention to our Lord's conversation with Nicodemus, I found that the Essay on this all-important 'Teaching of the Master,' comprehending, as it necessarily must, an examination of several controverted theological points, and also of other scriptural instructions connected therewith, would not be well adapted to the character of this practical paper. For this reason, and also because the former Essays continued for more than two years to be but little known or used by those for whom they had been especially prepared, the intention was abandoned. The Essay is finished, and I have had it on hand for some time, and shall perhaps publish it, if there be any probability of the necessary expense being paid.

The Parallel References, before mentioned, became so scarce in the course of ten years, that they could not be procured for the use of students. I therefore determined to prepare a second edition. As the particular bearing of the texts referred to was not always sufficiently obvious, I resolved to add such brief remarks as might be expedient, omitting any notice of portions which seemed of themselves sufficiently plain to any careful and intelligent reader. As I proceeded in this undertaking, I found it best to go somewhat more into detail. In less than a year a little book of two hundred and twenty-one pages was printed, the illustrations being limited to the Gospels and Acts. I dedicated it to the Alumni, and recommended its use to scriptural readers in general, and particularly to such as can not go beyond the English language. Since the appearance of this volume I have prepared similar notes, but somewhat fuller, on the Epistles to the Romans and Corinthians. Believing, as I do, that the most effectual way to acquire a right understanding of the New Testament is to examine it by the aid of parallel references, and thus make it explanatory of itself, I shall continue, as time and ability may allow, to prepare similar expositions of other leading epistles, in the hope that the time may come when both clergy and laity will, by this truly Protestant course, endeavor to teach revealed truth, and to engraft it, both in the minds and hearts of their younger brethren and children.

The last book, to the arrangement of which I devoted considerable time, made its appearance towards the close of 1860. It is simply the Gospels, in the form of the Harmony, which originated in the third century. In the Greek it had been before published, but never, so far as I know, in any modern language. It is called, *The Gospels, according to the Ammonian Sections and the Tables of Eusebius.* It consists of ten different parts. The first comprehends those portions which are common to the whole four. The second, third, and fourth contain corresponding selections from three: namely, Matthew, Mark, and Luke; Matthew, Luke, and John; and Matthew, Mark, and John. The five following are limited to those statements which occur in two only; Matthew and Luke, Matthew and Mark, Matthew and John, Luke and Mark, and Luke and John.

The tenth presents to the reader what is peculiar to each.

I have now brought down the particulars of my life, which may be supposed to be of any interest to my family and friends, to the summer of 1861, which finds me rather a feeble old man, in his seventy-second year, who can not reasonably expect to continue much longer in this world. May God, of his infinite mercy, prepare me for a better one, and when he shall be pleased to take me hence, may he receive me into his everlasting kingdom of glory, through the merits of my only trust and source of hope, the Lord Jesus Christ, the Saviour of sinners. I have had trials to be borne, some deep and permanent, but I have also had blessings without number to be thankful for. It is now nearly forty-three years since I became connected with the General Theological Seminary. I have not unfrequently felt that I was doing but little practical good in this position, and have regretted that I did not devote my life to the ministerial duties of a parish. At other times I have been much encouraged to believe that my efforts to instil revealed truth into the minds of young men, who were to go out into the world to preach the Gospel, have been useful. This feeling has been strengthened by witnessing on several occasions an increased attention to the truths of God's word, and an earnest endeavor to acquire clear views of them; by often receiving letters from young clergymen, expressive of their sense of the deep importance and practical utility of the study of the Bible as here recommended and pursued; and by witnessing the active exertions in the Lord's vineyard of many former pupils. Matters have, indeed, occasionally arisen which were very grating to my feelings; but these have been more than counterbalanced by expressions of kindness and respect on the part of students, which I could not have anticipated, and which I certainly feel that I had no right to claim. I will mention one which stands out prominently. After concluding my lectures to the Senior Class in 1855, as was my usual practice, with a few collects and the benediction, I was requested by one of the members to remain a few moments. On resuming my seat, he addressed me in the name of the class, which consisted of fifteen; and after expressing their regard in unmerited terms of thankfulness for instruction, he displayed to view a silver flagon, presented by them to the Chapel of the Seminary, in order to complete its set of communion vessels. It

12

was beautifully finished, with an inscription around the rim at the bottom to this effect, that it was presented by the Senior Class of 1855 to the Chapel of the Seminary, and as a token of regard for me. At the same time he handed me a letter, to which each member of the class had affixed his name, expressive of the feelings which prompted the act. The whole matter was altogether unexpected, and I could not reply at the moment in a manner at all adequate to my sense of their kindness. In my written answer I reciprocated it, with the hope that the great Head of the Church would accompany the ministerial efforts of each with his presence and blessing. The occasion was to me one of the most interesting and agreeable which ever took place during my connection with the Seminary.

CHAPTER XII.

EDITORIAL CONCLUSION.

Death—Funeral—Bishop Potter's Address—Notices of the Press
—Resolutions of various Committees, etc.

The preceding record of certain events with which the life of the Rev. Dr. Turner is associated will, of itself, be insufficient to convey a just idea of his character. The active, earnest Christian, the diligent and thorough scholar, the profound theologian, the ardent lover of truth, and its unflinching advocate through evil as well as good report, may stand out with more or less distinctness on these pages; but the whole man, as he was seen by his intimate friends and in his family, is very imperfectly presented. This could hardly have been otherwise, where the object of the author was so limited, and where a man so characterized by unconsciousness of self, was recording facts that pertained to his own history. A memoir from the hand of some friend, who knew him well and thoroughly appreciated his character, would contain much that could not be expected from his own pen, which would be both interesting and valuable to the reader. En-

dowed with quick and lively sensibilities, he
experienced and imparted great pleasure in
congenial society. All his domestic qualities
were of the most attractive and endearing character. He combined, in a rare degree, mascu-
line strength and womanly tenderness, a pure
and highly refined taste, with simple, unostentatious habits. His ever ready sympathies led
him to go "about doing good," wherever he
could relieve distress "in mind, body, or es-
tate." This is seen in his deep interest in the
Foreign Missionary work of our Church, and
in his active labors in its behalf, in his zeal in
preaching the Gospel wherever he spent his
summer vacations, and in the personal attention and practical relief which he bestowed so
liberally on the poor in the neighborhood of
his residence in New-York. He was cordial in,
and much "given to hospitality," and firm and
steadfast in his friendships. With a vivid and
just appreciation of the beauties of nature and
art, he joined a passionate love of music. The
indulgence of this taste was almost the only
recreation he allowed himself during his severe
labors and studies.

To this partial "record of a good man's life,"
the addition of what would be necessary to
present a complete view of his character and

labors would be out of place. The design of the narrative will be carried out, by appending a few facts, and some of the obituary notices and resolutions, which appeared in the Church press soon after his death. His labors, some of which he has sketched in this volume, were brought to a close a short time after the last page was written. He had returned from his usual summer retreat among the Green Mountains of Vermont, invigorated by its bracing air, and refreshed by that communion with the beautiful and sublime in nature which he so ardently loved and thoroughly enjoyed. One term of the Seminary year had passed in the pleasant discharge of his accustomed duties, and he was looking forward with satisfaction to the relaxation afforded by the Christmas recess, when the Master called him to the enjoyment of that eternal "rest which remaineth for the people of God." The high spirit which ever yielded unwillingly to the requirements of bodily infirmity, had been too exacting in its daily demands upon his nervous powers and strength, to leave much vital force in reserve for the struggle with disease. One week sufficed to "loose the silver cord;" but so gently was this done, that it seemed to be unmarked by himself, and almost by those around him. The mind, clear and unclouded, retained its supremacy on his bed of languishing. Its last energies were employed in giving directions, which proved to be final, to those whose advancement in piety and learning was the cherished object of so large a portion of his valuable life, and soon after he peacefully fell asleep in Jesus.

——•••——

I.

From the Christian Times.

The Rev. Samuel H. Turner, D.D.

WE take up our pen with a profound consciousness of our inability, by a brief and necessarily hurried notice, to do justice to the life, character, and labors of our distinguished brother.

The theological student and youthful friend of "the father of the American Church," his ministerial career stretching across a period of more than half a century, and nearly all of it indissolubly identified with the leading historical features of our Church, his official life alone would be a record too voluminous for these columns. And still, these very circumstances, as well as our personal affection for him as a tried Christian friend, demand more at our hands than an ordinary passing notice. A labored eulogy is not our purpose. It would not accord with his tastes, nor with the singular humility and absence of ostentation which marked his Christian course; but it is due to his exalted Christian character, and to the important position which he occupied so long, and filled with such honor to himself, that more than the bare mention of his departure should be recorded in these columns, which have been so often enriched by his gifted pen.

After reciting the outlines of his history down to 1836, the article continues :

It would be unsuitable to a notice like this, to follow up, with any thing like detail, the history of our revered and beloved friend beyond this point. It would involve the *secret*, and therefore the *real* history of the Institution with which he has been so honorably identified for forty-three years. It would, however, be an act of injustice to his memory and character, as well as to the cause of truth, if we failed to record the fact, that amidst the unlawful claims of official prerogative, the inroads of superstition and error, and even the harsh persecution of a bitter party press, he has commanded the respect of all, while he has remained unmoved and immovable in his principles, the same unflinching Protestant, fixed in his adherence to truth, the same Christian gentleman, calm and dispassionate in his position, because he knew that he stood upon a rock, and that the truth of God would, in the end, prove mightier than the craft, or malice, or power of man. For his unswerving fidelity to her principles, our Church owes him a debt of gratitude, of whose magnitude she will never be fully conscious.

Peculiarly qualified by mental constitution and early habits, for the work to which the providence of

God assigned him, he prosecuted it to the very last week of his protracted life, with unflagging zeal and patient industry. Largely endowed with common-sense; blessed with quick perceptions, a retentive memory, a spirit imbued with profound reverence for the inspired word; and uniting in a rare and happy combination a proper regard for human authority with independence of judgment, his numerous publications are not only a towering monument of his vast attainments in learning, but they present a mine of Scriptural truth, in which the Christian scholar may safely delve without any fear of its exhaustion, or of being led astray.

He was never idle. From the organization of the American Bible Society, he has been one of its warmest friends and most steadfast supporters; and he has evinced his interest in the Institution by the most unwearied labors in its behalf.

The same may be said of his interest in the Foreign Missionary operations of our Church, and of the value of his counsels in the Committee which is charged with the direction of the work. In addition to the numerous volumes which he has published, many of his valuable contributions to the cause of Biblical learning, and upon other kindred topics, have appeared anonymously, from time to time, in the religious quarterlies and magazines of the country.

For years, each number of the *Parish Visitor* has contained a column or more from his fertile and versatile pen, and the aggregate of his contributions to the *Protestant Churchman* would fill volumes.

Several modern and most of the ancient languages

in existence were familiar to him. Perhaps no man in this country or England combined such varied and extensive learning with such thoroughness and accuracy. We had hoped that the providence of God would spare him to place the results of his learning and labors in such a form that they might be available to the Church.

In connection with all this, he was not indifferent to general literature, nor an idle observer of the progress of the world in the arts and sciences. He had a keen and just perception and appreciation of whatever was beautiful in nature or art, in poetry and music. He was especially warm, genial, and confiding in his friendships. We shall ever esteem it as one of the greatest privileges of our life, that for twelve years we have been permitted to know him, to love him, and enjoy his confidence. As great as is his loss to the Institution which he has so long adorned; to the cause of truth, which he has so long vindicated and upheld; to the committees and societies which have so long enjoyed the wisdom of his counsels; and to the cause of Biblical learning, upon which he has for so many years shed such a continued lustre; the loss to his family and the circle of his intimate friends is even greater. So strong, mutual, and constant were their sympathies, that in separating from him, they seem to have lost a part of themselves.

They who have known and loved him must mourn over their loss; but their sorrow is tempered with joy, when the hand of faith lifts the veil from the unseen world, and the eye of faith gazes, enraptured, on the revealed glories of which he is a partaker.

12*

Blessed spirit! he has "fought a good fight;" his warfare is past, his race ended; he "rests from his labors" in those bright "mansions" where no lingering breath of the earthly tempest can ruffle the still waters of his eternal peace, or mar one note of praise, or dim one ray of light and love, as it shines, clear and unclouded, from the face of the manifested God.

—•••—

II.

From the Church Journal.

The Reverend Doctor Turner.

THERE is not one of the hundreds of the Alumni of the General Theological Seminary who will not learn with grief of the departure of the Rev. Dr. Turner. On the second Sunday in Advent he preached his last sermon, in St. Peter's Church, on "the last Judgment." During that week he was apparently in his usual health, and on Saturday afternoon said Evening Prayer in the Seminary Chapel; complaining of the coldness of the room, however, though the day was exceedingly mild. The coldness was the preliminary symptom of the disease which seized upon him during the night, and with several severe chills developed itself at last into typhoid fever. This gained daily upon his remaining strength, until, with little pain or apparent suffering, he departed in peace last Saturday evening, between six and seven o'clock.

Dr. Turner's name has been a household word with nearly all the active clergy of the Church, and from a time as far back as they can remember. The chair which he has filled—that of Biblical Learning and the Interpretation of Scripture—in the General Theological Seminary, has been occupied by him ever since the founding of the Institution. He has helped to train for the work of the sacred ministry a much larger number of persons than any other, whether bishop, clergyman, or layman, in the Church of America. And fully conscious of the greatness of the responsibility thus confided to him, no one has more conscientiously and industriously labored, day and night, to qualify himself for good service as a guide to the ministry in studying the unfathomable depth of God's word. This indefatigable labor he kept up through the whole of a professorship lasting nearly half a century; and down to the last week of a life prolonged beyond the ordinary span of threescore years and ten. With great natural strength and quickness of mind, he had so thoroughly imbued himself with the essential spirit of his own department— he had so cultivated the analytical and critical faculty in *every thing* connected with the interpretation of Holy Scripture—that the average result may be stated as that of soberness and general consent guarded on every side by common-sense, and fortified by a deep and various learning which left no source of information or illustration unexplored. Nor was his mind less characterized by keenness than by strength. None of his pupils will ever forget the relish with which he impaled the extravagance of some luckless commentator, ancient or modern, on the keen lance of his wit, and held up the wild enthusiastic vagaries of ignorance or fanaticism to the ridicule of the recitation-room. He has left many monuments of his learning, also, in the large and important volumes he has added from time to time to our treasures of Biblical learning. Nothing proceeded from his pen that was not devoted directly and chiefly to the elucidation and true understanding of Holy Scripture; and with patient courage and devotion he went on with volume after volume, though the demand for works which imbedded so much of the dead languages in their pages was never sufficient to reïmburse him for the outlay of publication, to say nothing of any profits from the sale. During the greater part of his long and laborious career, moreover, the Institution, with which he has been so honorably identified since its establishment, has been able to offer him but a very meagre support; and this year, the last of his veteran service, there was little prospect of his receiving any thing. It has been mainly through his own private means that he has supported himself while devoting the labors of a lifetime to the Church.

But aside from the strength and learning which were so admirably apparent in the class-room, there was another great quality which is not always found in combination with these. It was an exquisite tenderness and affectionateness of disposition, which rendered him acutely sensible to pleasure or to pain. Never have we known a man in advanced years more easily touched by the sight of another's sorrow, more easily melted into kindness at the tale of another's distress, more freely generous in supplying the necessities of those who were in want. Many of the clergy now serving in the vineyard can tell of acts of quick and open-handed liberality which they experienced at his hand, when struggling with early poverty in their efforts to qualify themselves for their high and holy calling—acts which will endear him to them as long as memory holds her seat.

But he has at length gone to his rest. The intimate personal friend of Bishop White; bearing the stamp of the earlier generation of American Churchmen in many things; long the colleague of the departed Dr. Wilson, and the yet surviving Dr. Moore, in an Institution which they all loved and served, but which he was the first to join and the last to leave; his departure removes one of the oldest of the landmarks from among us; and of all those, his sons in the Gospel, who stand about his grave to-day, and of all who hear of it at a distance too great to permit their presence in the body, there is not one that will not grieve over a father and a friend; they will grieve, not that he has gone home to receive his reward, but that they, on earth, shall see his face no more.

——•••——

III.

From the Church Journal.

"THE funeral of the Rev. Dr. Turner spoke deeply of the mingled affection and reverence with which he was regarded by all who had passed under his training hand. The nave of St. Peter's was nearly filled with a congregation mainly made up of *Alumni* of the Seminary, other clergy and students. The day was Christmas Eve, and when it is remembered how pressing are the calls of every parish at such a time on the care and attention of the clergy, it was no slight tribute to see so many of them gathered together, and not a few were those who had come from a distance on purpose to be present. The procession entered the church, led by the Bishop of New-York, the Faculty of the Seminary, and the Rector of St. Peter's Church."

The services were conducted by Professors Johnson and Mahan and the Rector of St. Peter's Church, and the following address was delivered by the Bishop:

"How strangely the lights and shadows of this our mortal life are intermingled! We find ourselves to-day in the midst of the holy place already decorated with its festive green—with its symbols of joy and immortality; but we come in the train of death, in the character of mourners. We suspend the preparation for our Christmas song, that we may perform the funeral rites over the mortal remains of our departed brother.

"And yet all is well! To us the loss is great. But this is a death in which there is no gloom. The good and faithful man, who has gone from us, had passed the threescore years and ten. His ministry had very nearly reached to the half of a century. His labors, in the great duty to which he had dedicated his life, had been extended beyond the usual term of active service for one generation. He had lived to hear again the Advent call: 'Now it is high time to awake out of sleep; for now is our salvation nearer than when we believed.' 'The night is far spent, the day is at hand.' He had preached in yonder familiar Chapel (the place that had known him so long, but shall know him no more) his earnest, tender Advent sermon—the Lord's coming to 'sit as a Refiner and Purifier of silver.' He had introduced another band of youthful pupils into the study of the holy Gospels. He had led them far on their way. He remained long enough to see the East beginning to glow with the light of the coming Nativity; and then gently, quickly, almost as it were by stealth, he departed to be with Christ; not staying to celebrate his birth here again amid the infirmities of the flesh and the shadows of this lower world—not waiting to gaze once more with the dim eye of faith upon the far-off manger of Bethlehem, but exalted suddenly to the blessed privilege of being delivered from the burden of the flesh, that he might be forever 'in joy and felicity with God.'

"It is not often that we are allowed to stand at a closing scene so full of all that can give a Christian content. It is not often that we have the privilege of looking back upon a life which has been so singularly favored with opportunities of usefulness, and in which those opportunities have been so faithfully and so largely improved. Forty-three years ago our departed friend began to be employed in giving instruction to candidates for the sacred ministry, and from that distant day to the present time his name has been conspicuously associated with theological education in the Church in this country. His pupils are numerously dispersed through every diocese of the Union; and I think I may confidently affirm that there is not one among them all who does not look back to his kind, paternal care with gratitude, to his character as a Christian gentleman, scholar, and teacher with affection and reverence. If you wish to see his monuments, look around at the ministry of the Church in this country. If you wish to listen to his eulogy, go visit any one of the four or five hundred of Christian pastors whom he has assisted in preparing for the Office and Work of a Priest in the Church of God, and you will hear him pronounce with deep feeling, that the days passed by him in the General Theological Seminary were among the pleasantest and most profitable of his life, and that no small share of the pleasure and profit of those days was due to the faithful and pleasant instruction, to the kind bearing, the judicious advice, the bright sunny character of the Professor of Biblical Learning and Interpretation of Scripture.

"It is now a little more than thirty-five years since I came to this city, almost a stranger, glowing with youthful ardor in the pursuit of knowledge, full of the hopes and fears with which every young man of any reflection must look forward to the work of the sacred ministry, and presented myself first to the Rev. Dr. Turner, to be examined and admitted into the Seminary. The impression of his kindness, of the cheerful courtesy and benignity of his manner, can never be effaced from my heart. At that early day I was privileged to see him frequently in his own house—a house not yet darkened by sorrow—a house brightened by the presence of one whose person and manners shed a grace and a charm over every thing about her. Through all the changeful years that have passed since that period, that cheerful, Christian home has been a solace and a refreshment to many a youthful student when weary, lonely, and discouraged. It has been to many a young man an image of what a Christian home should be, and may be, and at the same time it has warmed the heart to a more fervent love of the beauty of holiness. It is not for me to attempt to give utterance to the feelings of his Pupils now present. They have lost a Friend, a Father, a beloved Teacher, all in one. They will cherish the memory of his virtues, of his earnest, affectionate faithfulness; and they will endeavor to show themselves worthy to have been his pupils by striving to be followers together of him, and to walk so as they have him for an ensample. To speak in detail of the learning and the labors of our departed Brother, of his published writings, of the influence of his life on theological education in this country, and of his usefulness in other departments of Christian enterprise, would be unsuited to the solemnities of this hour, as it would be to undertake a task altogether too great for the opportunities afforded by this unexpected summons.

"Nor, my brethren, is there any need that I enlarge upon the lesson to be read in this event. 'Let me die the death of the righteous, and let my last end be like his.' Let my last look backward over the life rest upon a record as pure, as blameless, as full of the beauty of holiness, as full of trust in the blessed Redeemer, and as useful as did his. 'Blessed are the dead who die in the Lord. Even so saith the Spirit, for they rest from their labors, and their works do follow them.' We need not repine nor grieve that he rests in peace, that he has been delivered from the burden of the flesh, that he has been 'taken away from the evil to come,' that he has been advanced to the companionship of the blessed, that he is ever in joy and felicity with God. Look, my brethren, upon that coffin, and you shall see there such a promise of peace and blessedness as you can not see out amid the fiery passions and huge convulsions of the world. May that peace and that blessedness be ours in the hour of death, in the day of judgment, and through all the life that comes after the judgment."

On Christmas afternoon the remains, accompanied by the family and the Rev. Professor Johnson, were conveyed to New-Haven, where they were received by the Rev. Dr. Harwood, and borne to Trinity Church, in which they remained all night long. The next morning the journey to Cheshire, Connecticut, was resumed, where a company of clergy and friends received the body, and it was laid to rest beside the grave of his departed wife, who preceded him many years, but whose name, even to the last, he could never mention without tears.

After the funeral, on Christmas Eve, a meeting of the clergy present was held, presided over by the Bishop, of which the following is the official record:

St. Peter's Church, New-York, December 24, 1861.

The Clergy of the Protestant Episcopal Church in the Diocese of New-York, in attendance at the funeral of the Rev. Samuel H. Turner, D.D., Professor of Biblical Learning and of the Interpretation of Scripture in the General Theological Seminary, met after the service this day in St. Peter's Church.

The Right Rev. Horatio Potter, D.D., LL.D., D.C.L., Bishop of the Diocese, was called to the Chair, and the Rev. Thomas M. Peters was appointed Secretary.

On motion of the Rev. Dr. McVickar, it was

Resolved, That the Chair be requested to appoint a Committee of five, who shall prepare and publish, in the minutes of the proceedings, resolutions expressive of the sense of this meeting respecting the decease of the Rev. Dr. Turner.

The Chair appointed as their Committee, the Rev. Thomas H. Taylor, D.D., Rev. John McVickar, D.D., Rev. William E. Eigenbrodt, D.D., Rev. Alexander H. Vinton, D.D., Rev. Robert S. Howland.

The resolutions are as follows:

Resolved, That in the death of the Rev. Samuel Hulbeart Turner, D.D., Professor of Biblical Learning and the Interpretation of Scripture in the General Theological Seminary of the Protestant Episcopal Church in the United States of America, we mourn the loss of a brother of the most endearing qualities, and of an eminent servant of the Most High God, whose pure character and rare learning had long exerted a wide influence for the highest and best ends.

Resolved, That we recognize it as a cause for grateful praise to God, that in his wise goodness he should have blessed his Church, through so many years of time, with the bright example of a minister of his Word so beautifully fitted for the delicate and important duties with which he was charged.

Resolved, That while standing around his breathless remains, we will implore the Divine grace to enable us to emulate the virtues by which his character was enriched, and which still seem to shed their gentle, genial, and improving influence around us. Let us implore the Divine grace to enable us to be pure as he was pure, always loving, gentle, beneficent, and true; always meeting the ever-recurring calls of duty with promptness, punctuality, and cheerfulness, and never coming behind time in answer to the cry for instruction from the ignorant, for counsel from the young, and for comfort from the miserable. May we be enabled to give ourselves diligently, as he throughout his long life gave himself devoutly, "to the reading of the Holy Scriptures, and to such studies as help to a knowledge of the same;" and may we always, in meekness and single-hearted love of the truth, consecrate, as he did, the best fruits of our laborious learning to the cause of righteousness and charity in the world. While, like him, we hold fast with unwavering steadiness and consistency to our own enlightened convictions of what is right and true, yet in opposing the opinions of others, may we, like the learned man whose loss we deplore, "let our moderation be known unto all men."

Like him may we always cherish the great truth of "Jesus Christ and him crucified," as being, above all things else, near and dear to our hearts; and may we, like him, strive to show forth the constraining power of this our FAITH, by our weariless *works of love*, even unto our life's end.

Resolved, That a copy of these resolutions be sent to the family of the Rev. Dr. Turner, with the assurance of the sympathy of this meeting in their bereavement

On motion of the Rev. Dr. Eigenbrodt, it was

Resolved, That the Rev. Samuel R. Johnson, D.D., Professor of Systematic Divinity in the General Theological Seminary, be requested to prepare a discourse commemorative of the Rev. Dr. Turner, and to deliver the same at such time and place as the Faculty may determine.

Resolved, That the Secretary of this meeting be requested to give the clergy notice of such arrangement as the Faculty may make for the occasion.

The meeting then adjourned.

T. M. PETERS, Secretary.

Appropriate resolutions were also passed by the "Vestry of St. Peter's Church," by the Alumni Association of the Seminary, by the Protestant Episcopal Society for the Promotion of Religion and Learning, and by other bodies, which are not inserted in the following record:

The Faculty of the Seminary.

AT a special meeting of the Faculty of the General Theological Seminary, December twenty-third, 1861, on occasion of the lamented decease, after a brief illness, of the Rev. Samuel H. Turner, D.D., the late venerable Professor of Biblical Learning and the Interpretation of Scripture, and Dean of the Faculty, it was, on motion,

Resolved, That, in the departure of our reverend and beloved colleague in the fullness of his age and wisdom and unblemished piety, we deplore the loss to the Church of one of her ripest scholars and most devoted sons, at a time when his unimpaired vigor of mind promised still many years of efficient service; that the Seminary, in particular, sustains a loss difficult to be repaired, in one whose long, and faithful, and disinterested service of forty-three years has been distinguished by a thorough mastery of the rich and varied learning of his department, by instructions which have borne fruit in the life and doctrine of many of our most able clergy, by solid contributions to the stores of sacred literature, by unswerving loyalty to the cause of truth, and by a soundness of judgment in the discharge of his official duties, with a kindness, charity, courtesy, and sprightly and genial humor, which have endeared his memory to all who have been brought into contact with him; that the Faculty lament the loss of a colleague, brother, friend, and father, beloved for his guileless goodness of heart, revered for his pure and undefiled religion; that, in memory of all this, with humble submission to the Divine will, and with hearty thanks to God for the good example afforded in the life of our departed brother, we tender our cordial sympathy to his bereaved family.

The Standing Committee of the Seminary.

At a meeting of the Standing Committee of the General Theological Seminary, convened in the chapel of the Seminary on Tuesday, December twenty-fourth,

A.D. 1861, upon the death of the Senior Professor, the Rev. Samuel H. Turner, D.D., the following resolutions were unanimously passed:

Resolved, That the Standing Committee of the General Theological Seminary, in the name and on the behalf of the Board of Trustees, do hereby express their deep sense of the loss sustained by them and by the Seminary in the removal by death of the venerable and Rev. Samuel Hulbeart Turner, D.D., Professor of Biblical Learning and the Interpretation of Scripture, and, for the current academical year, Dean of the Faculty and Chaplain of the Seminary.

Resolved, That the long and faithful services of Professor Turner, both in government and instruction, during the life-long period of more than forty-three years, demand from the Trustees the strongest expression of regret and reverence, and the acknowledgment that his removal at the present time, even at the advanced age of seventy-two years, is felt by them as a severe blow to the Institution over which they preside.

Resolved, That the Trustees do now look back in thankfulness to the great Head of the Church that this distinguished Biblical scholar and teacher was so long spared to academic duties, alike learned and laborious, and in age pursued by him through many years of feeble health with a perseverance and self-denial of repose which nothing but the untiring zeal of a Christian spirit in the duties of his station could have supported him under.

Resolved, That in memory of one whose name has been from its foundation identified with the Seminary, its earliest and oldest professor, it be recommended to the Trustees that a suitable marble tablet expressing the same be placed on the walls of the Seminary chapel.

Resolved, That a copy of the above resolutions be addressed by the Secretary of this meeting to the family of Professor Turner, with the expression of the deep sympathy of the Trustees; and that, further, copies be furnished to the several Church papers for insertion, with a view to bring the same to the knowledge of absent Trustees, and to the Church generally throughout our country.

Attest. W. WALTON, Secretary *pro tem.*

The Foreign Committee.

EXTRACT from Minutes of a Special Meeting of the Foreign Committee, held on the twenty-fourth of December, 1861:

Whereas, Our Heavenly Father has been pleased, in His wisdom, to take away from us, by death, our revered friend and senior member of this Committee, the late Rev. Samuel H. Turner, D.D.; therefore,

Resolved, 1. That while, with the other members of our Church, we deplore the great loss which is common to us all, we are nevertheless truly grateful to our Heavenly Father that the Church was permitted to enjoy so long, in the person of our deceased friend, the admirable example of kindness, sincerity, and uprightness which distinguished him as a man; of earn

estness, spirituality, devotion, and faith, which characterized him as a Christian; and of fidelity to the
truth of Christ which marked his whole career as a
theological teacher. We are grateful that he lived so
long as to witness the large benefits of his labors, in
the character and success of many who, through a
term of more than forty years, had passed from his
faithful training into the ministry of the Gospel, and
who were ever ready to call him blessed; and that at
last, when his piety had grown constantly with his
years, and with his faculties undimmed, and his usefulness unabated, he was gathered to his fathers "like
a shock of corn, fully ripe."

2. That we mourn for our departed friend specially,
as a member of this Committee, who exhibited always
the truest zeal for the Missionary work, whose counsels were always wise, his measures discreet, and his
policy just and clear. We lament him as one who
habitually presided over our deliberations, and in
whose right-mindedness and impartiality we could
always confide, and whose dignified simplicity made
him revered as well as beloved.

3. That as the only demonstration we can now
make of our reverence for his memory, this Committee will proceed as a body to attend the funeral of our
deceased friend and fellow-member.

4. That a copy of these resolutions be sent to the
family of the late Dr. Turner, with the expression of
our joint and earnest sympathy.

Copy from Record.

S. D. DENISON,

Secretary and General Agent.

December 28th, 1861.

At a meeting of the Students of the General Theological Seminary, held December thirtieth, 1861, the following preamble and resolutions were adopted:

Whereas, It hath pleased Almighty God to re move our beloved and honored Professor of Biblical Learning and Interpretation of Scripture, the Rev. Samuel H. Turner, D.D., from the scene of his earthly labors to the glory of his eternal reward:

Resolved, That in his death we are bereft of an able, faithful, and conscientious guide in the path of Sacred Learning, and do mourn the sad vacancy now caused in the department which he so long and so ably filled.

Resolved, That while acknowledging and bowing in due submission to God's providence in this peculiar affliction, we are consoled and cheered by the memory of his long and meritorious labors in the promotion of Biblical Learning, by his uniform consistency and exemplary conduct as a minister of God, by his eminent and valuable services as a teacher of Theological truth, and by the comfortable assurance that he has made a blessed exchange from time to eternity.

Resolved, That we sympathize deeply with the Church in this removal of one of her most distinguished members, with our city and country for the loss of a true and faithful son of the Republic, with the Seminary for the loss of its oldest and earliest Professor, his name being identified with its very origin, and with the bereaved family who have so long been cheered by his presence, strengthened by his counsels, and encouraged by his example.

Resolved, That a copy of these resolutions be presented to the family of our honored and lamented Professor, feeling that in their loss we also have lost a friend and a father.

Resolved, That, in testimony of our profound regard for the person and character of the deceased, we wear the usual badge of mourning for thirty days.

Resolved, That a copy of these resolutions be communicated to the leading Church papers.

> G. A. WEEKS,
> O. W. WHITAKER, } Committee.
> H. H. COLE,

The American Bible Society.

AT the stated meeting of the Board of Managers of the American Bible Society, held January second, the Hon. Luther Bradish, Vice-President, presiding, the Rev. Dr. Brigham announced the decease, since the previous meeting, of the Rev. Samuel H. Turner, D.D., who for a long time had been a Life-Director of the Society, and a member of its Committee on Versions; whereupon it was

Resolved, That a Special Committee be appointed to prepare a suitable record of the event.

The Chair appointed the Hon. Walter Lowrie, and the Rev. Lot Jones, D.D., who, before the close of the meeting, submitted the following preamble and resolutions, which were unanimously adopted:

Whereas, In the dispensation of Divine Providence, the Rev. Samuel H. Turner, D.D., has been removed by death, the Board of Managers of the American Bible Society desire to place on record its appreciation of his character and services; therefore,

Resolved, 1st, That in all his relations to the American Bible Society, especially in his services for many years as an efficient member of the Committee on Versions, the deceased, by his uniform and consistent course, won the confidence and secured the esteem and love of all with whom he was thus called to associate.

2d. That this Board cordially sympathize with the family of the deceased, in the great loss it has sustained in the death of one so deservedly beloved and revered.

3d. That the foregoing preamble and resolutions be entered on the record of the Board of Managers, and a copy thereof be transmitted to the family of the deceased.

(From the Minutes.)

CALEB T. ROWE,
Recording Secretary.